BLISSFUL MASQUERADE

RUTHLESS DESIRES 1

ELIRA FIRETHORN

*To teenage Elira, who'd be horrified
that future her wrote this.*

Playlist &
Storyboard

Playlist:

A Little More - Rosemary Joaquin

i might like u - Boon

Temptation - Becoming Young

Cravin' - Stileto, Kendyle Paige

Apartment - BOBI ANDONOV

100% - Goldilox

Chills - Dark Version - Mickey Valen, Joey Myron

Do It for Me - Rosenfeld

Set Me On Fire - Estelle

Let Me - ZAYN

safety net (feat. Ty Dolla $ign) - Ariana Grande, Ty Dolla $ign

Paradise - Bazzi

Storyboard:

You can find Blissful Masquerade's storyboard by going to
pinterest.com/elirafirethorn.

Before You Read

Blissful Masquerade is a dark, erotic romance book intended for people over the age of eighteen. Please read over this content list to make sure there's nothing inside this book that could affect you negatively. Put your mental health first please!

Emotional: swearing, cheating (the FMC's ex, off-page), anxiety/running anxious thoughts, a mention of body shaming, internalized fatphobia (one scene), death of a child (off-page), and police corruption.

Physical: violence (fists, guns) and a mention of murder.

Sexual: dominance and submission, bondage, blindfolding, impact play, edging and orgasm control, over stimulation, and degradation. Everything is consensual.

Also, I purposefully left out most physical descriptors of most of the characters, including the main four. I know how annoying it is to read a book and realize the way you picture a certain character is completely off. So imagine them the way you want! You will, however, find the occasional description of a side character here and there.

(And to give credit where credit is due: I first got the idea from Ally Carter years ago when she intentionally didn't describe the love interest of her Heist Society series. I absolutely loved imagining Hale the way I thought of him, so I thought I'd give it a try with this series.)

The scenes in this book aren't meant to be a guide to BDSM or kink. This is a work of *fiction* and should be read as such.

blissful MASQUERADE

CHAPTER ONE

Wren

Note: This book contains some darker themes/kinks. Please flip back and read the Before You Read section if you haven't already.

I'm desperate.

And a little foolish.

That's the only explanation for the giddy feeling in my stomach when a familiar black SUV pulls into the parking lot. Why else would Fridays become my favorite day just because I get to see *them?*

Not that I'd ever do anything about it. That's a little too out of my comfort zone.

"Here they come." Ava elbows me, and I almost spill the coffee I'm making. "Ohhh, book boy looks *especially* nice today."

Groaning, I throw a lid onto the coffee cup, setting it on the pickup counter. "Order for Brooke," I call out.

I'm about to turn away, but just then, *he* steps through the front door. Tall, well-built, and with eyes that pierce the soul. And he's looking right at me.

Butterflies fill my stomach. Elliot Hayes is one of the three men who meets here every Friday morning for coffee. They're always dressed in sharp suits, almost too perfect to be real.

Over the months, Ava and I have caught them staring at me on more than one occasion. But Elliot is the one I talk to the most.

He approaches the counter, his friends—or coworkers, or whatever—behind him. "Good morning, Wren. Ava. Have a good week?"

Heat rushes through my body just from him speaking to me. He's looking at me expectantly, like he wants a *real* answer, not a fake, "Oh, it was fine."

Still, that's exactly what I tell him. It's a lie—my week was filled with too many encounters with my ex-boyfriend from hell. But that seems a little too deep and messy to explain to Elliot.

So I take their orders, noticing the way he narrows his eyes at my lie. *Was I really that obvious?*

But he doesn't say anything about it. Instead, he leans against the counter while I start working on their drinks. "Reading anything interesting?"

I pause as my smile fades. Every week, he asks me that exact question, and I always have an enthusiastic answer for him. Reading is my favorite pastime, and I usually average one or two books a week.

"I . . . well, I didn't really have time to read this week."

He frowns, but not in a disappointed way. If I'm not mistaken, there's concern etched into his features. "Too busy?"

"Something like that." I avoid his gaze. Normally, reading is my escape. And I had plenty of time to read this week—I just didn't have the mental energy.

Instead, I binged a new fantasy show every night until I fell asleep on the couch. Not the healthiest coping mechanism to deal with Adam's constant texts and calls, but it's not like it'll last forever.

And if it does—or if he puts me in even the *mildest* of reading slumps, I'll fucking kill him.

I just wish the asshole would take a fucking *hint*. You don't cheat on me and get away with it. I swear, good men only exist in books. *Specifically*, books written by women.

One of the other guys—Oliver Moore, the only one who doesn't take his coffee black—comes up beside Elliot. "Well, this guy had plenty of time to read. What's that book you recommended to him? *A Story of Two Cities? A Tale of Two Towns?*"

As Oliver claps him on the back, Elliot grunts. "How do you *not* know one of Dickens' most popular books? We literally read it in high school." With a grateful smile, he says, "Worth the reread."

Grinning, Oliver says, "I know it's *A Tale of Two Cities,* you fuckwit." Then he turns to me and winks. "I'm just pulling his leg. He's too book smart for his own good."

"Same with this one." Ava steps up to the counter next to me, jabbing my arm before handing Oliver his coffee. "She can recite historical facts in her sleep, but try to make a joke around her? It'll go right over her head."

"Oh, shut up," I mutter. That heat from earlier reappears, creeping through my veins. I turn away, finishing the two black coffees I'm working on before handing them to Elliot.

He just gives me a soft smile. "I hope you find some time to read this week, Wren. I know it makes you happy."

I open my mouth, searching for any words, but they all stay trapped in my throat. It's too overwhelming—the way he's looking at me, the sincerity in his tone and his gaze. Like he actually *cares*.

Ava snorts, reaching up to close my jaw. "She means thank you. Enjoy your drinks." Then she pulls me into the back, shaking me. "How did you ever manage to get a boyfriend?"

Blinking a few times, I glance back out front. Elliot is still standing at the counter, an amused smile playing across his face. God, it suits him well.

It takes me a few seconds before I'm able to tear my gaze away from his. "I mean, none of the guys I've dated have actually been that great."

Shaking her head, Ava sighs. "Still. Do you even know how to flirt?"

"Uh . . . kinda?"

As she lets out a frustrated sound, she throws her hands up in the air. "Hopeless. You're completely and utterly *hopeless,* Wren. Yet, somehow, it seems like all three of them have a crush on you."

My eyes go wide. The amount of embarrassment I feel as Ava waggles her eyebrows at me is impossible to put into words. For a moment, I wish I could dissolve into the floor.

Is Elliot still watching? I hope not.

"I don't know about all of them. Rhett seems a bit standoffish."

Ava frowns. "Which one is he? Because the two we just talked to were perfectly friendly."

"The third one. Kinda brooding? You were offended last week when he didn't laugh at your joke."

"Oh, yeah, he is a little standoffish." She taps her chin for a moment before shrugging. "Whatever. I still think you should invite book boy to the ball tonight. I'll happily give up my ticket if it means you getting laid."

"Shut *up,*" I grit out, glancing at the three men. They're at their usual table in front of the windows. Thankfully, that should mean they're out of earshot.

Originally, I was supposed to be going to the Valentine's Day masquerade ball with Adam. But when I broke up with him a few weeks ago, he gave me his ticket back.

But of course, he couldn't *just* give it back. He had to throw in something about how he thought the thing was "stupid" and he "didn't even want to go in the first place."

Still, Ava happily volunteered to fill his spot as my date, and she's been talking about it every day for weeks. I'm not taking this night away from her.

"No," I say. "It's Valentine's Day. And I'm not letting you sit at home alone. *You* need to find a pretty girl to take home."

She only glares at me for a second before relenting. "Fine."

My eyes wander back to the three men lounging in leather chairs and sipping their coffees. Rhett's cool gaze meets mine, and I freeze. He may be across the shop, but it feels like he's stolen the air straight from my lungs.

A faint smile crosses his lips—so faint I'm sure I'm imagining it—before I turn back to Ava.

I take a deep breath. Maybe Ava is right. If I can't even handle a man *looking* at me, I must really need some action in the sex department.

"Just promise me you'll *try* to find someone tonight. I don't want you to go home alone. That would be so sad." She gives me one of her signature, *I-know-what's-best-for-you* looks.

Inwardly, I wince. Because that was exactly my plan—have fun tonight, go home alone, and fall into bed. The idea of going home with a stranger isn't appealing to me, especially since that's how I ended up with Adam.

And I can't have a repeat of our relationship. I just *can't.*

Ava shoves me. "*Promise* me, Wren."

Rolling my eyes, I say, "Fine. I promise I'll try."

CHAPTER TWO

Wren

When Ava and I get to the hotel that the ball is taking place at, we're already a half-hour late. I wanted to leave early, but Ava insisted on coaching me on my flirting skills first.

We didn't get anywhere, though—whenever I tried to act sexy, we both just started laughing.

"This place is *gorgeous*," Ava says, looping her arm through mine as we enter the building.

"It really is," I murmur, taking in the place. It looks like it belongs in a classy European movie, and I can't help but feel like I shouldn't be here.

But Ava adjusts my mask, steps back, and beams. "You look absolutely stunning, girl. You're gonna kill it tonight."

I give her an uneasy smile. What I'm wearing is gorgeous, sure—it's a cream, low-cut dress covered in sparkly beadwork. The skirt isn't nearly as poufy as Ava's, and the sleeves hug my hands, leaving my fingers peeking out.

But as for the girl in the dress? She feels out of her element.

Why does it feel like everyone here knows my boyfriend cheated on me?

"Deep breaths, my friend," Ava says, running her hands along my arms. Then she's tugging on my hand, pulling me into the ballroom.

The room is classic—stone archways, a domed ceiling, the works. It truly feels like we're in a palace.

To top it off, the entire room is cast in blue and purple lighting, with crystal chandeliers catching the light. The whole place looks magical.

"Dance with me," Ava blurts, and before I can respond, she has me in her arms on the edge of the dance floor.

We spin through the crowd of elegant gowns and snug-fitting suits. As we do, Ava scans the room.

Bringing her gaze back to mine, she smiles shyly. "I may have told someone I was gonna be here tonight. Just seeing if she came."

I laugh. "Good thing I didn't let you give up your ticket. Damn, woman. You're a bad planner."

She levels me with a stupid grin. "At least I can actually function as a normal human being around my *crushes*."

Embarrassment coats my tone as I say, "Yes, I can! And I don't have crushes on any of them. I'm just awkward."

She giggles, glancing behind me. "You sure about that? Because I have a feeling you're about to lose your shit."

My eyes widen. *No. There's no way.*

She spins me around, and I freeze. Three men stand at the edge of the room, chatting and sipping amber-colored liquid from their tumblers. Their simple black masks may cover their faces, but I've spent enough time secretly observing them to be able to spot them anywhere.

The way Oliver throws his head back when he laughs. Rhett's calm façade that never lets up. And the habit Elliot has developed of running his thumb over his bottom lip.

God, it's so fucking hot.

"That's them, right?" Ava's voice is too loud, and I cringe. "It's gotta be. It's *gotta* be!"

"It doesn't matter." I steer us toward the opposite side of the room. "I'm just their Friday morning entertainment. No way they'll recognize me—or *care* if they do."

But a small part of my heart begins to hope, even though I wish it wouldn't. Elliot's eyes flash through my mind, filled with intention and such clear sincerity.

My stomach jumps as I recall that Oliver said he read *A Tale of Two Cities*. Elliot asked me last week what one of my favorite books is, and I blurted it out without thinking. I sobbed when I read it in high school.

The song ends, and we head to the makeshift bar set up in the corner. Ava orders something from the bartender, but I just stick with punch. No alcohol for me tonight—I need to stay in control.

Otherwise, I might wake up tomorrow and find myself with my *next* ex-boyfriend from hell.

We find an empty table and sit down. With a smirk, Ava turns to me. "They're looking this way."

"Well, maybe they're looking at you."

"Babe. My usual look *screams* lesbian."

As if on cue, Ava's face lights up, and she waves at someone behind me. I turn and see a beautiful woman with light brown skin and wavy black hair walking toward us with an equally enthusiastic look on her face.

I'm about to straighten out when my gaze snags on Rhett. And, for the second time today, he meets it—and takes my breath away.

"Hey, do you mind if I . . ." Ava gestures to the dance floor. She's already standing.

I smile up at her. "Go."

With a grin, Ava rushes into the arms of the woman she waved at. My heart swells. Ava deserves to be happy, and I can't help but hope she gets that chance.

Sipping my punch, I look anywhere except for the spot where Elliot, Oliver, and Rhett are. I can still feel Rhett's gaze on me, burning the exposed skin on the back of my neck.

I sigh. With Ava occupied, I've lost my dancing partner. And, unfortunately, most of the people here already came with someone to dance with.

The thought makes me think of Adam, which causes a frown to form on my face. To be honest, even if we'd stayed together, he'd probably be sitting at a table sulking on his phone.

Kind of like what you're doing right now.

A tap on my shoulder causes me to jump. I turn to find a middle-aged man looking down at me. His mask partially obscures his face, but I can still make out his light skin and salt and pepper hair.

"Now, what's a girl like you frowning for? Smile, honey. It'll make you so much prettier." He slides a hand onto my shoulder.

"You want something?" I say in an unamused voice, leveling this man with a *you're-a-pebble-in-my-shoe* look. I hope it shows even with my mask.

Damn. I really can be a bitch sometimes.

"I was hoping for a dance, seeing as your date must've abandoned you. What an idiot, am I right?"

Inwardly, I roll my eyes. As I'm about to reply, a deep, calm voice sounds from behind me.

"All of her dances are taken for the night, unfortunately."

With relief, I turn to see Elliot stepping uncomfortably close to this guy. Thankfully, he backs off, raising his hands.

"Sorry. Didn't realize she was taken." Then he walks off, probably to find some other poor, miserable girl who's found herself alone on Valentine's Day night.

I give Elliot a timid smile. "Thanks."

He chuckles. "Looks like you had it handled. Honestly, Wren. If looks could kill."

I frown, feeling my nose crinkle in the way Ava always says is cute. "He was being gross. And he couldn't take a hint." *Don't thank him again, don't thank him again, don't—* "Thanks again. Really."

"Glad I could help. Well, uh—" He tugs at his tie. "Just so you know, I meant what I said."

"Huh—what?"

"About all your dances being taken for the night. If you want them to be, that is." He shrugs, like my answer won't affect him either way, running his thumb across his bottom lip.

Goddamn.

I look around the room, as if an excuse to tell him no will be waiting for me. What I see instead is Ava, in the arms of her partner. She points two of her fingers at her eyes, and then flips them around to point them at me, mouthing, *I'm watching you.*

"Uh—sure. Wait, you're sure? Are you here with a date?"

Shaking his head, Elliot offers his hand, and I take it without hesitation. "We're here keeping an eye on Oliver's little sister."

I let him lead me onto the dance floor. When he puts his hand on the small of my back, I shiver.

"You cold?" Elliot frowns, and again I'm struck by the absolute sincerity in his expression.

Jesus. What is it about these men?

"N-no, not cold." I place one hand on his shoulder, letting him hold my other one in his. It's big and warm, and his grip is strong yet gentle.

"Why do I feel like that's the second time you've lied to me today?"

Fuck. I bring my gaze down, staring at his chest. His tie is thin, perfectly knotted at his neck. "Not the second," I say softly. "Promise."

He gives my hand a gentle squeeze, and when I glance back up at him, he's wearing a sad smile. "You weren't supposed to be here with Ava, were you?"

For a moment, I stop, stumbling as Elliot takes a step and pulls me forward. But he keeps me upright, his hand on my back steadying me.

"You're very perceptive," is all I can manage.

With a small shrug, he says, "I overheard a bit of your conversation this morning."

I have to fight the urge to ask him which part. "It's better this way. My ex is . . . something else."

"I'm sorry to hear that."

I inhale, breathing in his scent of sandalwood and oranges. It's a calming smell, which is exactly what I need right now. I just want to forget about Adam, but instead, the fear of ending up with someone exactly like him lurks in the back of my head.

Just focus on the present, Wren.

When I look back at Elliot, I find him watching me. His thumb runs across the back of my hand, and it shoots electricity up my arm.

"You look absolutely stunning, you know." His voice is low, and I stare as heat blooms in his eyes.

My lips part. I usually got a "nice" or "pretty" from Adam, if he complimented me at all. But *absolutely stunning?*

"T-thank you. You do, too. Although, I mean, you always do. With your suits and all."

He laughs. It's as mesmerizing as the stars. "Didn't realize you were looking."

"You didn't?!" It comes out *much* more incredulous than I meant, and he laughs again. All of my focus goes to his mouth as it curves into a beautiful smile. His lips look soft and perfect, like they're begging me to kiss him.

His arm tightens around my waist, and I realize *he's* staring at *my* lips, too. As he swallows, I watch his Adam's apple bob up and down.

Oh god. Is he going to kiss me? Is that what I want? Fuck, I don't know what I want.

The song ends, and Elliot brings us to a halt. My dress swishes at our feet, and I look down, breaking the moment.

I regret it instantly.

"Are you thirsty?"

With a small nod from me, we head over to the refreshments table. To my relief, Elliot keeps his hand on my back. We both get some more punch.

For a few minutes, we stand by the table, admiring the heart-shaped cookies with pretty designs from the icing. "You know," I say, turning back to him, "these cookies really are beautiful. In fact, this whole event is pretty classy, considering it's for one of the cheesiest holidays of the year."

Elliot laughs. "I'd have to agree with you there. Valentine's Day always seems so fake, you know? Forced."

"I swear, it's the one day couples actually treat each other like they're in love, just to go back to being shitty to each other the next day."

My words bring my mind back to Adam. To be honest, he couldn't even fake being a good boyfriend for a day. It was always, "Why do I have to get you flowers?" or, "It's a stupid holiday, it's not worth doing anything special for."

And it just made me feel like *I* didn't matter to him.

God. I have no idea why I stayed with him for so long.

Elliot raises his eyebrows, tilting his head and watching me closely.

"Oh my god," I murmur. My whole body feels like it's on fire. "I didn't mean to say any of that out loud. Oh, fuck."

Turning away, I cover my face with my hand. Now I look like a girl who's baiting him for sympathy and attention. *Dammit.*

"Hey." His voice is gentle as he takes my wrist in his hand, spinning me to face him. "Don't worry about it. He's obviously been on your mind."

"I wish he wasn't." I shake my head, sighing. "I'm so sorry, Elliot. I didn't want to dump any of that on you."

His arm slips around me, and I can't help but relax into him. He smells so *good.* "Let's get you a distraction, then. Me and the guys can keep your mind occupied."

I practically melt at the grin he gives me. And as he pulls me across the ballroom, I notice the undeniable heat building in my lower stomach. I know he probably didn't mean he and his friends would keep me occupied *that* way, but I can't stop my brain from going where it wants to go.

When we join the two men leaning against the wall, Oliver's face lights up. Rhett gives me a small nod, his eyes traveling over my body and making me squirm.

"You look like a princess," Oliver says, leaning in and kissing me on the cheek. He smells of vanilla and a woodsy musk scent that has my head spinning.

When his lips brush against my cheek, I lose all words. These three men have completely invaded my senses, and my body is drawn to them in a way my mind can't quite comprehend.

I'm sure it'll catch up eventually.

"Finish your punch, Wren," Oliver says, looking at me like I'm a toddler who just did something cute.

For some reason, I find myself doing exactly what Oliver told me to. When my cup is empty, Elliot takes it from my hand.

With a gentle push in Oliver's direction, he says, "Have fun."

Then I'm in Oliver's arms as he whisks me to the dance floor. I let out a giggle. Both his arms wrap around my waist, pressing me into his hard chest.

Finally, I remember how to speak. "You look nice, too."

"You're adorable," he murmurs, and I feel my world spin as he dips me backward. I grab onto his shoulders before realizing I don't really need to. This man is *strong*.

When he pulls me back up, I gasp in a breath. His eyes crinkle as he smiles. And right now, with the music filling my ears and his very presence dizzying my senses, I'm pretty sure there's nothing I wouldn't do to keep that grin on his face.

"So—uh, how do you know Elliot and Rhett? Are you friends? Business partners?"

"We met in high school, and we've stuck together ever since." One of his hands leaves my back, coming up to brush my hair out of my face.

"That's nice," is all I can manage.

His fingertips linger on my skin, skirting across my jawbone. When they fall to the sleeve on my arm, I let out a breath. No man's touch has ever affected me this way.

Geez. What is it about these guys?

Thankfully, I'm able to pull myself together more quickly this time. I smile up at him, and he returns it with an easy grin.

"Tell me, princess, what do you like to do other than read?"

"Hmm." I tilt my head toward the ceiling, frowning like I need to think about it. Finally, I say, "I like puzzles. And word games. Oh! And I love being outside. Well, when the weather is warmer. Snow and I don't really get along. It makes me anxious."

His smile fades for a moment at that last part, like he'd do anything to make sure I'm never anxious again. But the crack in his happy composure only lasts for a split second. "Puzzles, you say? And word games? My god, you really are just as much of a nerd as Elliot."

I clasp my hands behind his neck. "You're not?"

He shrugs. "School was never my thing. Although after watching Elliot and Rhett over the years, I must say, knowledge really is power. But there are plenty of types of knowledge—book smarts are only one of them."

What an interesting thing to say.

I'm about to ask what type of knowledge he possesses, but the song comes to a soft end.

"Thank you for the dance, princess." Oliver squeezes my waist before one of his hands slides into mine. It feels so natural, so *right,* that it takes me by surprise.

"Do you want more punch?" he asks when we re-join Elliot and Rhett. "Gotta make sure you stay hydrated."

For the umpteenth time today, my whole body feels like it's on fire. Because a man offered to get me *punch.* "Sure. Thanks, Oliver."

He grabs my cup from Elliot before disappearing into the crowd. I miss the heat of his hand in mine instantly, but before I can think about it too much, Elliot's hand has returned to the small of my back.

"Do you normally work weekends, Wren?" he asks.

I shake my head. Perks of being a long-time employee at the shop. It took years to get Saturdays and Sundays off.

As the next song starts, Elliot and Rhett exchange some kind of glance. The meaning is lost on me, but I swear I see a spark of nervousness in Rhett's eyes. Elliot, however, looks determined. Almost . . . hopeful?

When Oliver returns with my punch, I sip it slowly. Their eyes all flit to a young woman who hasn't left the dance floor all night. Her hair flows down her back, flying around as her date twirls her this way and that.

She must be Oliver's little sister.

I scan the room for Ava, finding her laughing at the refreshments table. She catches my eye and winks, waggling her eyebrows just like she did this morning. I almost choke on my drink.

"You good?"

"Great," I squeak out in between coughs. Someone takes the drink from my hand as I try to catch my breath.

Goddammit, Ava.

Finally, I clear my throat, and Rhett hands me back my drink silently. I chug it, trying to get rid of the discomfort still lodged in my throat.

When I glance back at Ava, she's laughing, and she can't stop watching me. I throw her a middle finger, taking a deep breath.

"That's your coworker, isn't it?" Oliver says.

Nodding, I turn so I'm facing away from her. I can't have another repeat of that incident. "We came together. I'm glad she found someone to spend the night with. I didn't want her to be lonely."

"And what about you?" The words come from Rhett. Cool, calm, with his head cocked slightly in interest.

"Me?" My voice is significantly more high-pitched than I meant for it to be.

Oliver elbows him in the chest. "Ignore this one. Wanna dance again?"

I laugh. "Sure."

He steps toward me, but Rhett grabs him by the back of the neck and hauls him away. Then he tugs me away from Elliot, my small hand clasped in his larger, calloused one, as he leads me to the dance floor.

When he finally turns to face me, that nervous look is back on his face. "Fuck. I don't actually know how—" He frowns, looking at me like I'm a puzzle he can't solve. For a second, I'm afraid he's going to abandon me.

"Just put your hands on my waist." I guide them, letting them settle above my hips. I rest mine on his chest. "To be honest, I'm not the best dancer, either. But most of the couples around us are kinda just swaying."

His eyebrows are knit together in concentration, but when he glances around the room, he seems to relax. Everyone else is taking a laid-back approach to dancing, choosing instead to focus on their partners.

I take a tiny step closer to him. He's so warm, and I can feel his heart pounding through his chest. There's so much tension in his body, I'm afraid he might explode.

"Hey." I keep my voice gentle, bringing one of my hands up so my fingers brush his cheek. *What am I doing. What am I doing. WHAT AM I DOING?!* "You're doing fine. And I'm happy to be dancing with you."

He lets out a stunned breath, but I feel him relax underneath my palms. He stares at me with such intensity I feel like I might burst into flames. When his eyes flit to my lips, I can't help but smile.

But he doesn't kiss me. All he says is, "Thank you. I'm happy, too."

He holds me closer, and we fall into a comfortable pattern, not moving too far from the spot we started in.

It gives me a moment to relax. And to let my mind catch up. It's far behind again, wondering what happened to the whole *keep your guard up, you're going home alone* thing. Because right now, I'd let any of these three men take me home in a heartbeat.

Even Rhett. I'm beginning to think his standoffish-ness is simply due to nervousness and social anxiety.

"Are you enjoying yourself?" I say, looking up at him. His jaw is still too tight, his shoulders a bit too high.

"I—social things—larger events—I'm not a big crowd type of person." He pulls me flat against him as Ava spins by with her partner, too drunk to care that they almost hit us.

My skin tingles at every point of contact with Rhett. Never mind that there are multiple pieces of clothing between us. My body has a strange reaction whenever one of these men touches me. I may not understand it, but I can't change it, and I'm not saying I *don't* like it.

It's definitely a new experience, though.

Rhett grunts when he looks down at me, finding my face mere inches from his own. His lips part, and I'm sure he's going to lean down and close the space between us, but then he straightens.

My face falls, and I have to look away. My whole body feels deflated, which is a surprise—I wasn't expecting this level of emotions for a man I've only ever chatted with.

When the song ends, Rhett's hands fall from my sides. But then he works his jaw, and his hand slides into mine. As other couples filter off the floor, we follow suit, heading back to Oliver and Elliot.

Almost instantly, Rhett drops my hand, taking his spot leaning against the wall. I let myself step closer to Elliot, and when my arm brushes his, he wraps it around my waist.

"Come with me for a moment," he murmurs into my ear.

He takes me out of the ballroom and into a quiet hallway. After a few steps, he backs me against the wall, placing both of his hands beside my shoulders. "I'm going to ask you a question, and I need you to answer honestly. Don't consider my reaction at all. Understood?"

With wide eyes and a smile I can't wipe off my face, I nod. This is it. This is *it*. He's finally going to kiss me.

His lips brush against the spot where my neck meets my jawbone. "I'd like to take you home tonight, Wren. Would you like that?"

"Yes," I whisper as my stomach does backflips. "But Elliot."

"Hmm?" He presses his face into my neck, inhaling. The action causes a shiver to shoot up my spine.

"I need you to kiss me first."

With a low chuckle, he pulls away to look me in the eye. One of his hands cups my cheek, and I lean into it with a smile.

"Preferably right now."

"Whatever you want," he says, leaning closer.

When his lips meet mine, I moan. He smiles against my mouth, pressing his body into mine. And when he finally, *really* kisses me, fireworks go off in my stomach. It's not until he pulls away and I find myself gasping for air that I realize I've grabbed onto his arms, pulling him toward me and not letting go.

"Would you like to leave now?" he says, his body still pinning me to the wall.

I groan. *"Yes."* I can feel how hard he is against me, and it's taking all my willpower not to grind against him in the middle of this hallway.

A slow smile crosses his face, and he kisses me again. "Go get your coat. I'll tell the others we're leaving."

With a nod that's probably too enthusiastic and a tad desperate, I head to the coatroom. I text Ava, letting her know I'm heading out. She sends me three eggplant emojis back, and I roll my eyes.

"Ready?" Elliot comes to stand beside me, reaching out and buttoning up my coat. Rhett and Oliver stand behind him, each shrugging on their own coats.

I nod, glancing at the other two. Are they coming with us? I suppose it makes sense that they all rode together. Before I can ask, Elliot's hand has returned to my back, and we head outside.

The cold air bites at my skin, and I shiver. But we're not even on the sidewalk for ten seconds before Elliot is opening the door to a dark limo and helping me inside.

Geez. This is fancy.

All three men pile in. Elliot settles in next to me, and Rhett and Oliver sit facing us. And that's when the awkward feeling hits.

The one that sits in the air, reminding me that I've flirted with all *three* of these men tonight, but I'm only going home with one of them.

A heavy feeling settles in my stomach.

They spent their night with me, and now they're leaving early because Elliot is. Am I the reason they're going home alone tonight?

God, I hope not.

My only response is a moan as he bites at the soft flesh of my breast. He tugs my dress down again, moaning at the sight.

"I need to get this thing off of you." He sits up, pulling me with him and searching for a zipper. When he finds it, he has it down in a split second. "Lift your hips for me, love."

I do, and he slides the dress and my panties off in one go. With a shy smile, I reach up and push his mask over his head. I grab onto his hair, pulling him into a kiss that knocks us both back down.

He rolls us so I'm on top, his hands squeezing my ass. "Stand up for a second. I want to see all of you."

His words make my lips part in surprise, but I find my body obeying his command before I even think about it. So I stand there, in front of his bed, completely naked except for my heels.

He leans back on his elbows as he takes me in. I can see the bulge in his pants, but he doesn't make a move to take his clothes off. The only skin of his I can see is his face, neck, and hands. The back of his left hand is covered with a tattooed rose that, for some reason, I've always found incredibly sexy.

I never thought his hands would be running all over my body. But now, I can't help but wonder what else he's going to do to me with them.

"If you're comfortable," he says in a low voice, "I want you to touch yourself. Show me what you like."

Any uneasiness in my body leaves. Has a man ever cared so much about what I'm okay with during sex? What I'm comfortable—and *not* comfortable—with? Just the fact that he's trying to respect my limits *makes* me more comfortable.

So I keep my eyes locked onto his as my hand snakes across my hip. I bring it downward until my fingers are slipping from my own arousal. As I find my clit, I let out a soft moan.

"Spread your legs for me, love. Let me see." His gaze is pure fire, burning so hot, for *me*.

I step to the side with one leg, circling my clit with my middle finger. My hips rock against my hand involuntarily as the sounds of my masturbation fill the air.

"*Fuck*. I can hear how wet you are for me, Wren."

My eyes slide closed, and my head tilts back slightly. I imagine his finger rubbing against my clit, sending sparks through my bloodstream. I shudder.

"That's it. Move your finger faster."

I do, and it causes the beginnings of an orgasm to build in me. I gasp when I feel him tweak one of my nipples. When I open my eyes, he's standing right in front of me, so close I'm surprised I didn't feel him.

He takes my hand in his, pulling it away from my body. He brings my fingers up to his nose, inhaling. Then he says, "Open your mouth," and slips my fingers inside. I suck myself off of them.

When I finish, he kisses the tip of my nose. "Good girl."

I let out a squeak. No man has ever called me *that* either, but it sends a fresh wave of desire through me.

As he breathes out a whisper of a laugh, he slides a single finger inside of me. The teasing action does nothing for the building tension in my body.

"*Elliot*."

"You're cute when you're desperate for me." He places a kiss on my jawbone, removing his finger and exploring. When he finds my clit, I gasp and grab onto his shoulders.

With my heels still on, I'm only a few inches shorter than he is. It gives me perfect access to his neck. My tongue flicks out and tastes his skin before I latch on and suck.

He groans, but he fists the hair at the back of my neck and pulls me away. "Am I not doing enough to drive every thought out of your head? You should've said something."

He captures my mouth in a kiss, holding my head still. It's not a normal kiss—it's all tongue and lustful, tiny nips at my bottom lip. Between his mouth devouring me and his finger shooting tendrils of warmth through my whole body, I can feel the beginnings of an orgasm building again.

I moan into Elliot's mouth as he prods my lips open with his tongue. It forces its way into me in an act that screams pure *dominance.* And when he pulls my head back, revealing the soft and vulnerable skin of my neck, the feeling only solidifies. Elliot is the type of man who could take control of my body and please me in ways I've never thought of before.

And I might just let him.

"I didn't think you could look any more perfect. But the way you look right now? I need to see you come, love. Are you going to come for me?"

I moan when he presses a line of soft kisses down my neck. He keeps going until his tongue flicks against one of my nipples. He sucks it into his mouth, and I swear my heart skips a beat.

He quickens the pace of his finger, and it only takes a few seconds before I'm screaming into his shoulder. My whole body shudders as he works me through my orgasm, until he sits on the edge of the bed and I collapse onto his lap.

"That was amazing," he says, biting the shell of my ear softly. "You looked so fucking beautiful."

All I can manage is a few pants and a clumsy kiss on his lips. Then, with a chuckle that warms my whole body, he sets me on the mattress.

"Let's get these shoes off of you." Sliding off the bed, he crouches in front of me. His fingers brush the insides of my thighs.

My eyebrows pull together. "You don't want me to keep them on?" He didn't take them off in the first place, so I thought he must've liked it.

He gives me a look. "There's absolutely no way I couldn't have noticed how these heels make your ass look. But the failings of women's footwear aren't lost on me, love. Your feet must be killing you." As he says the words, he takes my left foot in his hands and tenderly removes the heel.

He's not wrong. When he slides it off, I let out a sigh of relief.

Before he moves onto my other shoe, he kisses the sensitive spot next to my ankle, dragging his lips up my leg. When he reaches my upper thigh, I instinctually spread my legs farther apart. He flattens his tongue against my clit, giving me a single lick before pulling back.

I let out a frustrated sound, and he chuckles.

"Ready for more already?" He works off my other heel, repeating his action of kissing my ankle and running his mouth up my leg. Except this time, he doesn't lick my clit. "Good."

His arms snake under my thighs, wrapping around them, and he yanks me to the edge of the bed so hard that I fall back.

And then, finally—*finally*—he dives in. He sucks on my clit, flicking it with his tongue, and it takes everything in me not to scream. I bite my lip as he pulls away, looking up at me with hooded eyes.

"Please don't stop, Elliot. *Please*. You feel so good."

"Do I?" he murmurs, giving me a lick from my vagina to my clit.

I shiver. "Yes."

With a dark, satisfied smile, he leans in again. His tongue enters me, pressing against my walls, and I moan. Then he moves in and out, fucking me with his tongue like he did to my mouth earlier.

It's not as explosive as it would be if he was giving attention to my clit, but it still makes me lose my goddamned mind. His grip on my thighs tightens as he continues, groaning into me.

I bite my lip to stifle another scream as he finally brings his tongue to my clit. Oliver and Rhett are still here somewhere, and I don't want to make this awkward for them.

"Don't be quiet on their account. Trust me, love. They want to hear."

Elliot's words cause my stomach to tighten. "They—they do?"

He sucks my clit into his mouth before responding, releasing it with a lick. "Did you not see the way they were looking at you earlier? Let them hear that you're satisfied."

It's then that he releases one of my hips. As his tongue works me over, I feel two of his fingers sliding into me. I fall back onto the mattress with a loud moan.

He falls into a pattern, curling his fingers against my walls until he finds a spot that makes me cry out. With a smirk, he goes back to licking my clit. And with his fingers inside of me, hitting that same spot over and over, and his tongue completely wrecking me, I can't help it. I scream his name so loudly that I'll probably never get over the embarrassment in the morning.

He adds more pressure with his fingers, sucking on my clit, and I come so hard that I scream again. He leans back, watching me, moving his fingers in and out.

"Elliot, oh god—*Elliot,* I—" I give up on trying to form a coherent sentence. Instead, I groan when he pulls his fingers out of me.

Panting, I prop myself up on my elbows and watch as he sucks my arousal off his fingers. His eyes slide closed as he moans.

"You taste better than I ever could've imagined."

My head is still spinning, so I don't move when he crawls on top of me. He kisses me, his tongue entering my mouth so I can taste myself. When he pulls away, I run my hand over his belt, settling on the bulge in his pants.

"Your turn?" I say breathlessly.

With a smirk, he climbs off of me and stands. "Not yet. I'm nowhere near finished with you, love."

I crawl to the edge of the bed, grabbing onto his shirtsleeve. "At least take this off? I want to see you." Without thinking, I kiss the palm of his hand, and then each of his fingers. When I get to his thumb, I take it into my mouth and suck. He groans.

After I release it, his hands move to the top of his shirt, undoing a few buttons. I can see the outlines of a tattoo peaking through, but I can't make out what it is yet.

"More," I say, and it comes out sounding like a whine.

He raises his eyebrows, but before he's able to retort, there's a knock on the bedroom door.

My eyes widen. Rhett and Oliver know *exactly* what we're doing. So why would one of them come knocking on the door? Unless . . .

Elliot lowers himself to a crouch in front of me. With an even gaze, he takes my hands. "They want to watch."

Oh.

He stares at me, gauging my reaction. "Is that okay with you?"

I swallow, my eyes flitting to the door. *Is it okay with me?* They watched us earlier, and it was outside of what I'm used to doing, but I'd be lying if I said I didn't think it was hot.

Besides, I'm the reason Rhett and Oliver came home alone tonight.

No, I think to myself. *If you're going to do this, it can't be out of a feeling of obligation. You won't be able to stay in the moment.*

"Wren." Elliot squeezes my hands, and I expect him to press me for an answer. But instead, he says, "If it makes you even the slightest bit uncomfortable, I want you to say no. *Need* you to say no."

I hesitate, thinking this through. Was this their plan all night? Flirt with me, have one of them bring me home, and then the other two get to watch? The thought feels dirty.

But as I look at Elliot, at the relaxed sincerity on his face, I know that can't be true. I have a feeling Oliver and Rhett knocked on the door with absolutely no expectations at all.

"Are we scaring you?" His voice is gentle.

I shake my head, smiling down at him. "Just needed to think. They can watch."

Elliot narrows his eyes at me, probably looking for a tiny bit of hesitation. But he must be satisfied with what he finds, because he gets up to open the door.

Before he takes more than two steps, though, I stop him. "I have one condition, though."

He turns, waiting.

I have to fight the urge to look away. "I want to go down on you."

He laughs. "Deal."

He opens the door, and Oliver and Rhett file in. They've taken off their masks, but they're still in their suits. The only indication that either of them has relaxed at all is Oliver's loosened tie.

"Damn, Elliot." Oliver gives me a once-over, winking at me. Rhett's eyes linger on me as well, but he stays silent as he settles into a chair in the corner of the room.

For a moment, I'm confused by Oliver's reaction. But then I realize I'm still panting. I probably look as dazed as I feel, too.

With a shy smile, I slip off the bed and settle onto my knees. Elliot walks over, cupping my chin, and I look up at him. The fire in his eyes matches the hunger I feel coursing through my whole body.

I undo his belt, sliding it off and placing it on the floor. Slowly, I unbutton and unzip his pants, keeping my eyes on him the whole time. I stroke him through his boxers before slipping my hand beneath his waistband and pulling his dick out.

He's larger than Adam, and I eye him nervously. Am I going to be able to fit him in my mouth? For a moment, I hesitate, but then I realize that I actually *want* to choke on his cock.

Heat curls in my lower belly as I lick him from base to tip. He groans, pulling my hair back and keeping a firm grip. I take his tip into my mouth, wrapping my right hand around him and stroking.

With every bob of my head, I manage to take more of him in. His fist tightens around the hair at the base of my neck, and I moan. When he hits the back of my throat, I gag but don't pull back, letting myself adjust to him.

"I'm going to take control now, Wren. Are you ready?"

My eyes go wide.

"You can take it, love. You're already doing so well."

I moan in response, relaxing and moving both of my hands to his thighs for balance.

"That's it," he whispers, pulling out a few inches. "Ready?"

I give him a small nod, my gaze flitting up to his face for a moment. His eyes are half-closed, foggy with pleasure. When he slides back into me, they close all the way.

He starts off at a slow pace, most likely for my benefit, before he speeds up. It doesn't take long for my jaw to ache and tears to fall from my eyes, but I don't care. There's something about the way he's holding my head and fucking my mouth that makes me never want him to stop.

"*Fuck,*" I hear Oliver mutter. His voice is strained.

The reminder that he and Rhett are watching sends a wave of butter-flies to my stomach. It must have a similar effect on Elliot, because he groans.

His thrusts slow, and I expect to feel him come, but instead he pulls out of my mouth. I moan in disappointment, opening my mouth and trying to lean forward, but he keeps his grip on my hair firm.

"Stand up."

I scramble to my feet, losing my breath when he kisses me. His hands brush away my tears, and I can't help but wonder if I have mascara running down my cheeks.

Elliot turns me around, pressing my back to his front. I can feel his erection, and I grind my ass against him. I don't think I've ever cared so much about seeing—and *hearing*—a man come undone. Yet I'm ready to do anything to experience Elliot coming. In me, on me, I don't even care.

But he has other plans.

"Spread your legs."

I do.

"Now let them watch you come apart from a single one of my fin-gers."

For the first time since Elliot turned me around, I actually *look*. And what I find are two men staring at me with pure, unadulterated lust. The thought of getting on my knees for both of them crosses my mind just as Elliot slides a finger over my clit, and I shudder.

When Elliot slid my dress off in the limo, there was a split second when I felt too vulnerable. But now, with Elliot holding me on display for Rhett and Oliver, the feeling of being exposed to them only makes me more wet.

Elliot makes a deep, dark sound as he feels it. My head falls back onto his shoulder as he works my overly sensitive clit back to life. It doesn't take long before I'm a mess, sputtering half-sentences and tugging my hair with my hands. I don't know what to do with them, and I can't figure out where to put them that doesn't make me feel self-conscious.

I squeeze my eyes closed when Elliot slows his finger. An orgasm was *just* beginning to build, but now it's fading away. I bite one of my fingers, stifling a frustrated groan.

But then two hands wrap around my wrists, pressing them to soft fabric. I open my eyes to see them against Rhett's chest. He's watching me closely, searching for any type of resistance. But the way he's en-trapped my wrists against his chest feels so *right*.

My gaze locks with his, and his piercing stare goes straight to my heart. He's looking at me like a starved man staring at a feast. "Rhett," I whisper, watching as he raises an eyebrow. "Rhett, kiss me. Please."

The words flow out of my mouth so naturally that what I'm really opening myself up to doesn't register until I've already said them. But I don't care. I need to feel this man's lips on mine.

Rhett doesn't hesitate. His grip on my wrists tightens, and then he pulls them over my head and holds them there. When his lips finally crash into mine, Elliot's finger speeds up again. I cry out, Rhett absorb-ing the sound in his mouth.

His free hand creeps up my body, sliding in between my breasts and tracing my collarbones. Then it wraps around my throat, his thumb and forefinger squeezing ever so slightly.

All of a sudden, everything is too much, and I explode. My knees go weak, but I find myself held up by Rhett's grip on my wrists and Elliot's arm wrapping around my waist.

Rhett doesn't release my mouth, instead running his tongue over my bottom lip as I moan into him. My hips buck as Elliot's finger shoots fireworks throughout my whole body, and he stops when I start whimpering.

I gasp, falling against Rhett's chest as he lets my wrists slip out of his hand. He holds me for a second before tensing and stepping back suddenly. The lust in his eyes disappears, replaced by an unreadable façade, before he backs away.

Elliot keeps me upright, stroking my hair as I catch my breath. But his hold on me loosens when Oliver comes up next to us. I barely register him before the room tilts as he picks me up and carries me to the bed.

When he settles on the edge, placing me in his lap, I rest my head on his chest. He kisses my hairline with a chuckle. "You look tired."

Shaking my head, I straighten. "I can take more."

His lips part as he looks me over. "Tell me, princess, do you want me?"

I moan as I nod, leaning in and kissing him. His lips are soft, and the way he kisses me is gentler than the other two. While one of his arms is wrapped around my waist, his free hand cradles my face like I'm the most precious thing in the world.

Groaning, Oliver pulls away. I can feel how hard he is. "I need to feel you come around my cock, princess."

His words make me pause. I haven't had a random hookup in years, and the topic of protection is always awkward. The guys never want to wear a condom, and the whole thing ends up being a mess.

Planting a kiss on my neck, Oliver says, "We're clean, Wren. Or we can wear condoms. Whatever you're comfortable with. Are you on birth control?"

I nod, my eyes moving from one man to the next. All three of them have on a patient expression, and it makes my heart squeeze. Do they really mean it? They don't mind either way?

And should I believe them just because Oliver says they're clean?

"Mmm. No, you shouldn't." He chuckles as my eyes widen at the realization that I was thinking out loud. His lips drag across the skin of my shoulder. "We can show you proof if you'd like."

"I—I don't have proof."

"You don't seem like the lying type, love." Elliot steps forward, brushing my hair out of my face before kissing me. "And we really are okay with using condoms."

I let out a breath, relaxing into Oliver. "Why don't you get the paperwork." I watch as Oliver grins.

"Sure thing, love."

After Oliver sets me down, he and Elliot both disappear out of the room. Rhett pulls up something on his phone, hesitantly handing it over to me. Our fingers brush, and it feels electrifying.

I scroll through his test results silently before handing his phone back to him. He swallows, tugging at his tie. That nervousness that I saw in his eyes at the ball is back.

"You okay?" Just like I did earlier, I stand, bringing my fingers up to graze his cheek. The skin-on-skin contact with him makes me shiver.

With a frown, he shrugs his jacket off and drapes it over my shoulders. "Yes." But his voice is tight, his movements too sharp.

My face falls, and a slight ache begins to build in my chest. He's been tense all night, and now, looking back over their visits to the coffee shops, he's always been distant.

Heat creeps through my veins as I remember how I begged him to kiss me. "You don't want me."

He lets out a strangled breath. As I take a step back, he takes one forward. Tears—of rejection or embarrassment, I'm not sure—fill my eyes. But he grabs my hand, placing it over his erection.

"Does this feel like I don't want you?" Then he moves my hand to his chest, right over his heart. It's thumping so hard I'm afraid the man might have a heart attack. "What about this?"

I frown. "But you—"

"Forget about it."

"But—but Rhett, you—"

"Jesus, Wren." He grabs my face in both hands and slams his mouth against mine. He bites my bottom lip like he's angry at me for making him want me, but then he slides his tongue into my mouth like he needs to devour me.

When he pulls away, my knees are weak. That insatiable lust is back in his eyes, and when a tear falls onto my cheek, he licks it away.

I want to ask him what's going on in his head, but I have a feeling he's not going to tell me. And as he steps away from me, the guys return. Elliot has tucked himself back in, which is disappointing, but I guess I wouldn't want to walk around the house with my dick hanging out, either.

After looking over their test results, Oliver pulls me back onto his lap and peppers my neck with kisses.

"You're sure you don't mind that I don't have proof?" I ask. It comes out in between shallow breaths as Oliver tweaks my nipples with his fingers.

"We don't say things we don't mean, love." Elliot gives me a heated look. He's leaning against his dresser, watching as Oliver explores my body.

I swallow, deciding that's a good enough answer. My hands go to Oliver's shirt as I work on the buttons with shaky fingers. Unlike Elliot, he lets me slip it off his shoulders. I moan as I take him in, kissing the butterfly tattoo on his chest. It's the same one Rhett has tattooed on the back of his right hand.

"Let me get my pants off, princess." With ease, Oliver lifts me off of him and onto the bed. He stands, undoing his belt and pants in record time. He shoves everything to the floor before pulling me to the edge of the bed. "Lie back and close your eyes. Just focus on what you feel."

I do what he says, but I struggle to keep my eyes closed. I want to watch as he slides into me. Cocking an eyebrow at me, he lines himself up at my entrance.

Oh god.

"What did I say, princess?"

I groan. "Eyes closed."

"And relax. Your head shouldn't move from the mattress. Understood?"

With a dramatic sigh, I do what he says. But I can't help the smile that plays across my lips.

When he finally enters me, I let out a groan. He does too, his hands pushing on my thighs to open me even more to him.

"Oliver," I moan, and I can't help it. I open my eyes, raising my head to watch him. He grunts when our gazes meet, and I reach out so my fingers can brush against his hard stomach.

"Close your eyes, Wren." The words come from Rhett. When I look over at him, something stirs deep inside of me. His tie is gone, and he's undone a few of the buttons of his dress shirt. But what really catches my eye is the way he's pulled himself out of his pants and is stroking himself.

"Oh god," I whisper.

I feel myself clench around Oliver. He slams into me harder, and I know I should listen, but I can't manage to tear my eyes away from Rhett.

With an amused huff, he stalks toward us and climbs on the bed. "You just can't seem to listen tonight, can you?" He grabs my arms and pins them to the bed.

I let out a giggling squeal as he leans over me.

"Close your goddamned eyes, Wren."

For a second, I contemplate disobeying him. What would he do if I keep my eyes on him? But on second thought, I decide to listen. Because I really *don't* want anything to distract me from the way Oliver feels inside of me.

So I let my eyes slide closed, relishing in the way he's grinding against my clit. He fits so well inside of me.

"I love how wet you are for us, princess." He pulls out, and I feel his fingers bringing up some of my arousal to my clit.

I barely notice one of them—probably Elliot—grabbing a couple of pillows, or how he lifts my hips and slides them underneath me. But what I absolutely *do* notice is the new spot Oliver hits when he slides back into me. I cry out, but the sound is muffled by Rhett's mouth covering mine.

My back arches when Oliver's thumb finds my clit. With the way he's moving in me, and with Rhett's mouth on mine, I don't think I'm going to last much longer.

"That's it, princess. I need you to come for me." Oliver's voice is tight, like he's struggling not to come. I want to peek at him, but I don't think I'd even be able to get my head up, considering the way Rhett is kissing me.

So instead, I focus on the sensations these men are pulling out of me, and how much I love the freeing feeling of Rhett holding me down.

When I come, it's with a scream. Rhett pulls away, and while I keep my eyes shut, I can only imagine him watching me. The thought makes me come harder.

I hear Oliver grunt, and with a gasp my eyes fly open. I watch as he falls apart, feeling him finish inside of me. He falls forward, catching himself with his arms. For a moment, he looks at Rhett, and I swear they're about to kiss—and I *want* them to. But then Oliver leans down, kisses me lightly, and straightens.

When he pulls out of me, I let out a long breath. My whole body is shaking, and I've lost count of how many orgasms I've had tonight.

"Relax, Wren." Oliver squeezes my thigh. "Give yourself a minute to recover."

I lay back, taking a few deep breaths, and my eyes land on Rhett—specifically, his cock, which is only mere inches from my face.

I wiggle up, trying to get close enough. When I do, I lift my head and lick the precum from his tip.

He grunts in surprise. "Fuck, Wren. You're insatiable."

"Please," I gasp, trying to tilt my head to take him in. But it's an awkward angle without him helping.

"You're sure you can take more?" he says in a teasing tone, running the tip of his cock across my lips.

I let out something that could only be described as a little growl, and he laughs. It sends a wave of warmth through me, reaching my bones.

"Open up, sweetheart."

I do, moaning as he adjusts himself and slides into me. He moves in and out slowly, filling me as he lets out a string of curses. My fingers dig into his sides as he bottoms out, hitting the back of my throat. When I gag, he pulls out, watching me closely.

I suck on his tip, and his eyes shut while he groans my name. One of his hands palms my breast, his thumb rolling over a pebbled nipple.

"Tap my thigh if you need me to stop. Okay?"

His gaze rips right through me, and I manage a little nod. Then he leans over me, kissing my stomach before flattening his tongue against my clit.

I let out a strangled scream, causing him to groan. But he continues his assault on my clit, sucking and licking it like it's his lifeline. The entire time, he fucks my mouth with slow, even strokes.

God, how is his body not shaking like mine? How can he manage to tear me apart with his tongue while he's in my mouth?

As if to answer my question, he lets out a deep groan and pauses with just his tip in my mouth. His tongue circles my clit, bringing me *so* close to the edge. But I'm not ready yet. I want to come *with* him.

So I suck on his tip, trying to move my head up and down in the slightly awkward position.

He swears, one of his hands gripping my thigh. I keep all of my focus where he seems to like it the most, and he punishes me with tiny, quick strokes of his tongue against my clit.

It does me in. As he slides into me again, I let out a deep, gurgling moan. He shudders, and his whole body tenses.

Yes, yes, yes!

He moves to pull out of me, but I grab his hips to hold him in place. I want—*need*—to feel him come in my mouth.

With a grunt, he does, and I feel every hot spurt on my tongue. He pulls out, twisting to fall on his ass as he watches me. I open my mouth, propping myself up on my elbows and letting some of his cum drip out of my mouth. Then I swallow, licking it off my lips.

"Fuck," he says on an exhale. "That was hot."

I crawl over to him, and he pulls me onto his lap with a small kiss. His calloused hand runs up and down my back, and I settle against him with a small sigh.

For a few moments, we stay just like that, and I can't help but smile at how relaxed Rhett is. I have no idea what was bugging him earlier, but it doesn't seem to matter anymore.

The mattress sags. I glance over to see Elliot sitting on the edge of the bed. He's pulled his cock back out, and he's stroking himself with slow, steady movements.

While still clinging to Rhett, I lean over and kiss him. It pulls a moan out of Oliver, and I giggle.

Elliot takes my face in his hands, kissing the tip of my nose. "How are you feeling, love?"

I give him a quick kiss before he straightens. "Like I can handle you." I know I'll probably be sore in the morning, but the thought of *not* being with Elliot like I've been with the other two tonight doesn't sit right with me.

He lets out a soft chuckle, running a hand over my hair. "Do you trust us, Wren?"

I let myself mull over the question. No man has ever taken his time with me like these three have. They've always gone straight for what they want. But not Elliot, Oliver, and Rhett.

Is that a good enough reason to trust them? Probably not. But they've been so caring, and patient, and *sincere* all night. Including before we left the ball.

Maybe I shouldn't. Maybe it's a foolish thing to do. But as I glance between the three of them, it hits me: I really, *truly* do trust them.

Chapter Four

Elliot

I watch as Wren thinks over my question, biting her lip in a way that somehow makes my dick even harder.

Good, I think as she glances between the three of us. *I want her to take this question seriously.*

With a small smile, Wren looks up at me and nods.

I smile back. "And how much experimenting have you done in the bedroom, love?"

Her smile falls, and she looks away. "Not that much. I wanted to, but . . ." She shrugs. "Doesn't matter right now."

I watch her closely, looking for any sign that we're making her uncomfortable. Tension in her shoulders, too-wide eyes, closed off posture. But I find nothing except a hint of sadness that I know has nothing to do with us and everything to do with that motherfucker who broke her heart.

"I'm going to tell you a few things I've observed tonight. Tell me if I'm right or wrong, okay?"

She nods again.

My fingers brush across her cheek, because I can't help but touch her. She's like a fucking drug. "You seemed to like it whenever Rhett restrained you. Specifically, when he raised your arms above your head, and when he pinned you down when Oliver was fucking you. Am I correct?"

She gives Oliver a heated glance, and he returns it. Then, looking back to me, she says, "Yes."

"Pretty sure you liked it when I choked you, too." Rhett nudges her jaw with his nose, and I smile at the show of affection. He's done well tonight.

Wren's eyes widen, and a shy smile appears on her face. "Yeah." Then she turns to face me, an expression of cautious curiosity on her face. "What do you want to do to me?"

I smirk. "Tie you up."

Her lips part as the words register in her brain.

"You'd be able to tell me to stop at any time. And I won't tie you up for very long. Not this time, at least." I watch as heat ignites in her eyes at the thought of doing this again. "But I only want you to agree to this if you're one-hundred percent on board."

She doesn't even hesitate. "I want you to."

Fuck me.

"Get on your back."

She obeys, but not before giving Rhett one last kiss. Taking deep breaths, she watches me take out some soft ropes from a dresser drawer. Then I get to work tying her up. Every time my skin touches hers, she shivers. Rhett grabs his jacket from the floor and drapes it over her.

Jesus. I don't think I've ever seen him care this much about a woman since we were kids. Although it makes sense. We've all been drawn to Wren since the second we set our eyes on her.

I tie her so she's laid out spread eagle on my bed. She looks perfect against the forest green comforter, even with Rhett's jacket covering her.

Once I'm finished, I stand at the bottom of the bed. "Warmed up?"

She nods, so I remove Rhett's jacket, tossing it to him. She squirms under my gaze as I unbutton my shirt and shrug it off. Her eyes snag on the butterfly tattoo on my ribcage before I yank the rest of my clothes off.

When I crawl on top of her, she's smiling and taking my body in. I let her before I lean down and kiss her. Rhett's taste is still potent in her mouth, and I groan.

I pull away before she's ready, and she tries to sit up but can't. With a half-laugh, half-moan, she lets her head fall onto the mattress. *Good.* I want her relaxed.

I squeeze her breasts. She watches my face, gasping when I lean down and take a nipple into my mouth. I alternate between sucking and licking it until she's writhing underneath me. Then, with a mischievous smile, I move to her other breast and do the same thing.

"Elliot," she groans, trying to roll her hips against my erection. But I keep myself just out of her reach. "Elliot! *Please,* Elliot."

I release her nipple, straightening. *"Please* what, love? You're going to have to be more specific."

She lets out a desperate huff, her eyes flaring as she realizes that I'm going to make her beg for it. "Fuck me?"

I raise an eyebrow.

"Please fuck me?"

"You're going to have to be more convincing than that."

She lets out a tiny growl that can't be categorized as anything other than completely adorable. "Please Elliot? Please fuck me? I've wanted to feel you inside of me all night, and I *need* you to."

I smirk. "That's more like it."

It only takes me a moment to line up with her entrance. I feel her tense with expectation, her hips trying to rock me into her. So I sit like that for a moment.

Maybe it's cruel. But I've craved her for so long. She always felt so untouchable behind the counter at the coffee shop, with her infectious smiles and giggles. I never thought this moment would come. And now that it's here, I want to see her as desperate as I've been for months.

"Elliot," she yells. She tries to wiggle closer to me, but she can't.

Oliver snorts out a laugh as we watch her struggle.

"You're both ridiculous," she murmurs, looking toward Rhett for any type of solidarity. But he's barely holding back his smile, either. She sighs, slumping onto the bed.

And that's when I slam right into her. She screams, her back arching off the mattress, and I do it again. To my great satisfaction, she goes back to forming half-sentences, begging me not to stop.

So I don't. For a minute, anyway. But when I feel myself getting close, I slow. She lets out a groan of frustration.

Then I look to Oliver, and then to Rhett, before my gaze lands back on Wren. "Can we blindfold you?"

She nods without hesitation. Oliver grabs his tie from the floor, crawling onto the bed next to her head. With a trusting smile, she closes her eyes as he slips it over her eyes, wrapping it around twice before tying it at the back of her head.

Oliver gives her a gentle kiss before hopping off the bed. I slide into her again, and I hear her whisper a little, *"Fuck."*

I rub my thumb against her clit, and she gasps. God, this woman is so fucking *sensitive,* I have no idea how she's lasted this long.

It only takes a minute or two before I'm close again. But based on her shallow breaths and the way she's clenching around me, she is, too. I catch Oliver's gaze, nodding to her body, before doing the same thing with Rhett.

They're on her in seconds. Each of them takes a nipple into their mouth, and she screams. Her wrists pull at the restraints as she comes, and I have to hold her hips down while she pulls me over the edge with her.

She shudders as she feels me filling her, moaning when we all pull away from her at the same time. I take a moment to recover while Rhett and Oliver work on her restraints. When she's able to sit up, she does, pushing the makeshift blindfold off her face. The second she sees me, she holds out her arms.

I climb onto the bed and pull her onto my lap. She's shaking and panting as she wraps her arms around my neck.

"You took that so well, love." I kiss her hairline. "So well."

She moans into my skin before glancing at the other two. I can't help but laugh. They're both hard again already.

She lets out an exhausted breath. "I—I can't . . ." Her head falls against my chest.

Oliver chuckles, leaning onto the bed to kiss her on the shoulder. "We know, princess. We know."

. . .

Wren moans as I carry her into the bathroom. Rhett and Oliver have already said goodnight. And then they drew her an Epsom salt bath while I got her a glass of water and she recovered in the bedroom.

Setting her on the tile floor, I hold her steady until she gains her balance. "Pee. And then you're going to soak in the bath. It'll help with the soreness."

She smiles up at me, sated and sleepy, and I can't help but kiss her. Then she disappears into the small toilet room while I step into the giant tub.

When she joins me, I pull her in between my legs, with her back settled against my stomach. She sighs, her head resting on my shoulder. "Tonight has been amazing, Elliot."

I kiss her hair. *"You're* amazing, love.“ And I mean it. I never expected her to last as long as she did. Hell, I didn't even expect her to come home with me, even while I was asking her to. The idea of her in my bed seemed too far off, too much of an untouchable fantasy.

And now she's here, her naked body pressed against me. Her breaths have evened, and I'm pretty sure she's already fallen into a light sleep.

"We really wore you out, huh?" I mutter into her neck. She lets out a soft moan.

I stroke her hair while we soak, staying absolutely still. When the water cools around us, she wakes with a shiver.

"Ready for bed?" I murmur in her ear.

She nods, standing slowly. I step out of the tub first, grabbing a fluffy towel and drying her off. Goosebumps cover her skin as I finish, kissing each of her inner thighs.

I dry off quickly, noticing her noticing my erection. I can't keep my dick calm around her.

After hanging our towels up, I turn to find her with her arms outstretched. I pick her up, stifling a groan when she wraps her legs around my waist.

As I carry her to the bed, she grinds against me, all while yawning into my shoulder. I can't help but let out a laugh. "Do you want me to fuck you to sleep, love?"

She pulls away to look at me, smiling sleepily. Then she nods. "No one's ever done that to me before."

I watch her as my chest shakes with silent laughter. Is she serious? Is it even possible to *literally* fuck someone to sleep?

She kisses me sloppily, and I realize I'm about to find out.

Once we're settled under the covers, I pull her into a spooning position. I prop her top leg up, giving me room, and slide into her.

Fuck. How is she already so wet?

I fuck her nice and slow, not even trying to build her up to an orgasm. She sighs as I hold her to my chest.

It doesn't even take a minute before her body sags against mine. Soft snores fill the air, and I have to stop myself from laughing.

After cleaning both of us off with a warm washcloth, I find one of my old T-shirts and pull it over her frame. She mutters something before settling against the pillows again.

Some type of emotion expands in my chest, one that I haven't felt toward many people. I clamp it down. Tonight has been too perfect to fuck it up by telling her how I really feel. It doesn't matter. The fact that she's in my bed is a miracle all by itself, and I'm not stupid enough to walk into this with any type of expectations.

So after a minute of staring at her form under the blankets, I kiss her on the cheek. "See you in the morning, love."

CHAPTER FIVE

Wren

I wake with a gasp. My body is shaking, and I have to blink back the tears in my eyes.

The images of my nightmare are already fading from my mind, but that doesn't stop the panicked feeling in my chest.

Where am I? What's going on?

Light. I need light.

As I reach for the lamp on the nightstand, a familiar scent of sandalwood and oranges hits my nose. And as the light clicks on, pushing back whatever imaginary monsters are lurking in the dark, I relax a bit.

Last night's events flood my memory. It's not enough to completely calm my nerves, though.

I turn, reaching for Elliot, but I find the bed empty. My heart sinks. *Where could he be?*

The sound of soft piano music wafts through the bedroom. Is he still up? The clock on the nightstand tells me it's a little after three.

I frown. I know I should go back to sleep, but my heart is pounding too fast, and my mind is too alert. If I lie back down in the dark, I'll just get anxious and panicky.

That's how this always works.

With a sigh, I slip out of bed and go to the bathroom. There's a brand-new toothbrush set out on the counter, and I smile at the thoughtful gesture.

After peeing and brushing my teeth, I head toward the sound of whoever's playing a piano. But I don't make it past the bedroom door before my feet freeze.

The hallway is dark—*dark* dark. My skin prickles as my heart rate picks up again. I've never gotten over my childhood fear of the dark, and it always intensifies when paired with the nightmares I get when I'm stressed.

Wait. Why am I stressed again?

Oh, right—Adam.

I flick the bedroom light on and open the door wide. It floods part of the hallway with a soft, yellow glow. Then, with a cautious step outside, I peer at the surrounding walls for a light switch.

Of course, I don't find one.

My fingers dig into the doorframe. *You can do this. You're not a little kid. There's nothing that's going to hurt you.*

The sounds of a faint conversation drift by, along with the music. I'm pretty sure it's coming from downstairs.

Maybe if I run fast enough, I won't get too scared.

It's a bullshit thought, and I know it. But I can't just stand here forever, and going back to bed until I have an anxiety attack is somehow even less appealing.

So, with a deep breath, I take off down the hallway. The light from the bedroom fades as I turn around a corner. If I'm remembering correctly, the stairs are over here somewhere.

The music is getting louder, and I hear someone laugh. My breathing gets heavier as I take the stairs slowly, too afraid of falling to go quickly.

When I reach the bottom, the back of my neck is prickling. It feels like someone—or *something*—is going to snatch me into the darkness.

But I can see a faint light coming from farther in the house, so I take off again. When I finally burst into the room, the music stops immediately.

"Princess?" Oliver stands from the piano bench, stalking toward me when he sees the panic on my face.

I run to him, jumping into his arms with a sob. My legs wrap around his waist as he holds me. "I woke up alone, and everything was so dark. I—I got scared."

His arms tighten around me as he moves to the piano bench and sits back down. One of his hands runs up and down my back while the other holds me securely. "Fuck, Wren. You're shaking so badly. Is this just from being scared?"

I bury my face in the crook of his neck. "I get nightmares when I'm stressed."

Embarrassment creeps through me. I'm acting like a kid. And I knew this was going to happen tonight—why did I just magically forget when Elliot asked me to come home with him?

"That's awful," Oliver murmurs. "Do you need anything? Water? Food? A blanket?" His fingers skim my bare legs, and I realize I'm in nothing but a T-shirt.

I frown, thinking. *Do* I need anything? Normally when this happens, I just turn on a light and read to distract my mind until I'm tired again.

But then I remember something, and I gasp, clinging to Oliver. "I heard voices!" I scan the room, looking for Rhett or Elliot. But all I find are a few empty couches and chairs and a lit fireplace.

Oliver just smiles softly, stroking my hair. "Voices? Or *a* voice? I was on the phone, Wren. There's no one else here."

But I can't stop looking around, peering into every dark corner in the room.

Oliver grabs my face, turning me to look at him. *"Wren.* You're safe. I wouldn't let anything happen to you. I promise."

My body finally relaxes as I look into his eyes, so genuine there's no way I couldn't believe him. "You were on the phone," I murmur.

He nods. "With Elliot. He's out working with Rhett. They're on their way home."

What a short shift. And what an odd time to be at work.

Oliver glances away. "I . . . can't really sleep when they're gone." He rubs the back of his neck.

So they *do* live together. "You don't work with them?" I run a hand over his hair, letting the feeling ground me.

"No, I do. But we didn't want to leave you here alone." He kisses the tip of my nose.

I tilt my head, watching him. It's sweet—although this conversation is bringing up about ten more questions about what type of relationship these men have with each other.

"You're still shaking." He lifts me up and carries me to the couch, where he settles me on his lap with a blanket. "Are you tired?"

I sigh. My heart rate has returned to normal, and the feeling of the darkness chasing me disappeared the second Oliver's arms wrapped around me. "I think I'm getting there."

He kisses my forehead, and I quickly move to capture it with my mouth. He smiles against my lips. "Try to relax. I promise you won't wake up alone again."

So I do. With my head settled against his chest, I close my eyes. The sound of his steady heartbeat in my ear soothes me, and it's not long before I'm drifting off to sleep again.

Chapter Six

Oliver

After the guys make it home, I'm able to get a few hours of sleep. But when the sun rises, so do I.

I settle into my usual morning spot—a small table in the sunroom, overlooking the front yard—and pull up an article Rhett sent me last night.

The house is quiet. Elliot took Wren back up to bed after he showered, and he won't wake until around ten. As for Rhett, he disappeared to one of his usual hiding places, probably to brood. I don't think he quite knows what to do with the effect Wren is having on him—on all of us.

As if my thoughts conjure her, she steps into the sunroom. She's still only dressed in Elliot's T-shirt, with her hair pulled into a bun on the top of her head.

"Morning, princess." I sip my coffee before smiling at her, setting my phone down. The article can wait—it's boring, anyway. "Hungry?"

She nods, stretching her arms up over her head with a yawn. Just as I thought, she's not wearing anything underneath that shirt. Probably because I'm an ass and hid her panties from her last night.

What can I say? I was hoping for a moment like this.

She realizes I'm watching her and drops her arms.

"C'mere." I uncross my legs and pat on my lap. When she straddles me, planting a happy kiss on my lips, I have to stifle a groan.

"Thank you for comforting me last night," she whispers, rewarding me with another kiss. Then her head drops. "I'm kinda embarrassed now. But the dark—I swear, the older I get, the more I'm scared of it."

"We all have our worst fears, Wren." I run a hand down her back.

"What's yours?" She tilts her head just like she did last night when I had her in my arms on the piano bench.

I pause. Sure, there's the usual shit—spiders, bugs, heights, etc. But nothing—and I mean *nothing*—compares to the physical pain in my chest whenever I realize I could lose one of the people I care about the most.

It feels strangely intimate to tell that to Wren, but I do anyway. I did have my dick buried in her last night, after all.

She listens to me, nodding, and we fall into silence while we watch each other. She missed some of her hair when she put it up, and the strands frame her face. It makes her look like an angel in the morning sunlight.

After a moment, she swallows. Then she blurts, "I have a question."

"Shoot."

"Do you—do you do this often?"

I grin. "Spend my mornings with beautiful women on my lap? Unfortunately, no."

She rolls her eyes. "That's not what I mean. Do you guys . . . take women home often?"

Ah.

"We've all brought our fair share of people home separately."

She bites her lip, and I wait for her to ask what she *really* wants to know. "But never . . . together?"

I chuckle. "No. You're the first. And from the looks of things, the last." I watch her closely as her eyes fill with relief and then unease.

Fuck. That probably didn't come out right.

"Not like that, princess." I palm her back in long up-and-down strokes. "I don't think we'll ever be able to top last night with someone else. And I think the guys agree."

I mean it. I really, truly do. The three of us have been together in one way or another since high school. And we've *never* shared a woman together. Never wanted to—until Wren.

Her eyes go wide as she smiles shyly. I kiss the embarrassment right out of her until she's panting when I pull away. Knowing I put that light in her eyes makes my heart swell with pride. But there's a hint of nervousness as well.

Which, if I'm being reasonable, is understandable. I basically told her that she's so fucking special to us that no woman could ever have the same kind of chokehold that she has on us.

Well, that's *sort of* what I said.

Regardless, it's a lot for the poor woman to take in.

My stomach growls, and she giggles. "You haven't eaten breakfast yet?"

I give her a devious smile. "Oh, I'm about to."

She perks up. "What are you gonna have?"

"Something I've been wanting to taste for a long time but haven't been able to."

Her eyebrows knit together as she gives me an odd look. "Uh, okay? What's that?"

Goddamn. She really is as oblivious as Elliot. "You, princess."

Her mouth falls open in a shocked smile as I lift her onto the table in front of me, careful not to spill my coffee. I hand it to her, and she takes a sip as I spread her legs and get a good look at her. She's fucking perfect.

Holding her legs, I dive in like a man starved. And, when it comes to her, I kinda am. Finally, I get to taste her. She lets out a squeak, and I hear my coffee mug *clang* on the table.

"Oh god, Oliver." One of her hands fists my hair, and I welcome the pain as I eat her out.

I go gentle on her clit, figuring it's still sensitive from all the attention it got last night. When I delve inside her with my tongue, she rocks her hips into my face. I nip at her skin lightly, and she gasps.

"Hold still, please. I'm trying to enjoy my breakfast."

She giggles, and the sound lights up my goddamned soul. I trace my tongue in a circle around her clit a few times.

"Oliver, please—why—*ohhhh*." She shudders when I finally suck it into my mouth.

I relish in the satisfaction of being able to take away her ability to form full sentences, just like Elliot did last night. I tease her with the tip of my tongue, going *too* lightly, and she lets out a frustrated noise.

"Do you want to come, princess?" I slide a single finger inside of her.

She's panting desperately, but she still raises an eyebrow at me with a sassy look on her face. "What do you think?"

I do everything in my power to stop my grin from taking over, but I fail miserably. "You better wipe that attitude right off that pretty face of yours. Only good girls get to come in this house."

She scoffs playfully. "Oh, so you're the type of man who leaves a meal unfinished? How wasteful of you."

"Only when the meal talks back."

She rolls her eyes. But when I pull my finger out of her, she gasps. "No! No, I'll be good."

I shrug, grabbing my coffee and taking a sip.

"Oliver! Please. I promise I'll be good."

"And how will you do that, princess?"

"I—I'll do whatever you want. Please just make me come, Oliver."

With a chuckle, I slide my finger back inside. Her head falls back when I curl it against her. "Anything?"

"Yes." Her voice is hoarse from being made to wait.

"Well, that's good. Because I have a few things in mind. First off, tell me something you've always wanted to do in bed but haven't yet."

She straightens, her eyes big. Then shyness takes over, and she looks away. But when my finger begins to slowly inch out of her, she gives in. "I've always wanted to try—uh . . . words." Her eyes squeeze shut.

"Words?" I curl my finger into her again, watching her writhe. "It sounds like this would be a good time for you to use some, princess."

She makes a flustered sound that I have to stop myself from laughing at. Then, finally, she spits it out. "Degradation!" She winces. "But nothing too mean."

I reward her with another finger sliding into her. She's too in her head to give me examples. My mind goes over last night, at how she reacted to what we said to her—specifically any type of praise.

"Tell me, princess, do you want us to call you our pretty little slut?"

Her eyes darken, and she nods. I reward her by sucking her clit until her legs are shaking.

"Our own personal fucktoy?"

"Y-yes. Please."

I add a third finger, finding her sensitive spot and hitting it over and over again. I want to keep exploring her likes and finding her boundaries, but this isn't the time. I don't want to push her and accidentally ruin the moment by triggering her.

So I lick her clit and say, "Good girl," watching her eyes roll into the back of her head. And then I work her until she comes so hard that she can't help but scream my name.

"Damn, princess. You might've woken Elliot with that one."

"Oh, no!" She claps a hand over her mouth, and I'm surprised by the genuine concern on her face.

Is it possible that she cares about us as much as we care about her?

I squeeze her thigh. "Probably not. The man could sleep through the end of the world."

She relaxes, and her hand drops to the table.

My mind snags on an idea. "Don't you have something to say?"

"Huh?" She looks at me with confusion as she closes her shaking legs.

I lean back in my chair, leveling her with an even gaze. "I just made you come so hard you screamed the whole house down. I think a 'thank you' is in order."

She bites her lip as she realizes what I'm doing. "Thank you, Oliver."

"I believe I deserve some type of payment."

She nods with big, innocent eyes that I can't help but think *aren't* as innocent as they look. "Whatever you'd like."

I slide my pants and boxers down my legs. "Ride me. Show me how grateful you are for your orgasm."

She lets out a breath as she scrambles from the table and straddles me. I help her line me up with her entrance, and then she sinks onto my cock with a moan.

She grabs onto my shoulders, her fingers digging into my shirt.

"Are you sore?" My hands rest on her hips, ready to pull her off of me at the slightest sign of pain.

She wiggles her ass, settling. "Not really. I think I just need a second to adjust." She takes a deep breath, tilting her head back, and I feel her relax around me.

I plant a kiss on her neck as she works her way up and down, rolling her hips to grind against me. Her deathgrip on my shoulders loosens.

"Is it okay if I go slow at first?"

I nod, leaning back so I can get a better view of her. "Take off his shirt. Right now, you're mine. All mine."

She obeys, tossing the shirt to the floor. With a smirk of satisfaction, I take in her body as she picks up the pace slightly. Her breaths are shaky, and I can't help but move my hips to match her movements.

The feeling rips a moan from my throat, and she smiles.

"Do you like pleasing me, princess?"

She nods, her smile growing. She picks up her pace more, and I match it. This time she moans, and her eyes slide shut.

Fuck. I don't know how we're supposed to let her go. What if she wants to leave after breakfast?

Then you'll take her home.

"Oliver, I—" Her head drops to my shoulders, trying to keep up with my thrusts. "Fuck," she whispers.

When did I take control? I can't pinpoint the exact moment.

Her whole body goes rigid, and she cries out into my shoulder. I can feel her clenching around me as she comes.

I slam into her once more before finishing inside of her. She shudders, her lips finding mine. Then she collapses against my heaving chest as she tries to catch her breath.

"That was quite the show."

Wren jumps at Rhett's voice, straightening. I have to turn to see him, but he's directly in her line of sight.

With a laugh, he steps forward and kisses her. "You actually didn't see me, did you?"

She squirms. "I—well, I was pretty distracted." When her gaze focuses on the erection straining in his pants, she looks up at him. "Do you..."

But he shakes his head. "The sound of you coming undone is all I need right now. Well, that, and—" Rhett grabs my hand, sucking the three fingers that were inside of her moments ago. His tongue runs over each of them until every trace of her is gone.

When he releases me, I grin at the way Wren's mouth is hanging open slightly. She lets out a small squeak when Rhett kisses her again, saying, "See how good you taste? No wonder we can't get enough of you."

"Jesus Christ," she whispers.

"Nope. Just a couple demons, making sure you end up in hell with us for all of eternity." He brushes his fingers against her cheek. "Now. Did Oliver at least feed you before he fucked you?"

"Hey! I was getting there."

Wren giggles, turning back to give me a warm smile. "I am pretty hungry."

He helps her put on her shirt, and when he pulls her off my lap, there isn't an ounce of jealousy in me. Instead, my heart fills with happiness at the way Rhett lets Wren wrap her arms around his neck. He kisses her cheek with a grin.

It's been far too long since he's opened up to someone like this.

I just hope he doesn't fall too hard.

. . .

During breakfast, I can't take my eyes off the beautiful woman sitting at our kitchen island. Everything she does is perfect, even when she's stuttering out something that makes her feel awkward.

It makes me want to strip her back down to nothing and worship her until she begs me to stop. And based on the way Rhett can't stop looking at her either, he feels the same way.

That's probably what causes the words to come out of my mouth. I know how I feel, and I know how Elliot and Rhett feel as well. And I'm just not ready to let her go yet.

Still, even as I say them, I feel like I'm handing her a gun and giving her permission to shoot me.

"Stay the weekend."

Rhett almost chokes on his orange juice. I'm grateful Wren doesn't have anything in her mouth, because based on the look on her face, she would've had a similar reaction.

"All weekend?" She looks between me and Rhett with surprise.

That was the stupidest thing you've ever said, Oliver. She probably has plans.

"Yes."

She blinks. Tilts her head again.

Rhett's hand slides across the counter, taking hers. "Only if you want to, sweetheart. But if you're doubting whether we want you here for the next two days, trust me—we do."

Her thumb rubs across the back of his hand, and she looks between us again. "I don't have any clothes. Or my facewash, or—"

"Perfect excuse for a shopping trip!" I grin, and Rhett throws me a look that says, *Give her a chance to say no.*

"A shopping trip? I can just run home."

"How about both?"

She rolls her eyes. "I work at a coffee shop, Oliver."

It takes a moment for the meaning behind her words to register. "No, you wouldn't spend a thing. We'd be spoiling you."

The corners of her lips turn up as she takes a bite of her breakfast. "I've never had anyone spoil me before, let alone three gorgeous men."

"Gorgeous, huh?" I wink at her.

"You guys really don't mind?"

I bark out a laugh. *"Mind?* If you say no, I'll spend the weekend heartbroken and miserable."

"Oliver," Rhett snaps. This look says, *I'm going to fucking strangle you.*

If Wren is put off by Rhett's harsh tone, she doesn't show it. Instead, she just laughs. "I'll stay. Just as long as you'll let me leave if I decide that I want to."

I give her a grin. "Of course, princess. And I won't actually be heartbroken if you decide to. Promise." *Lie.*

As she takes a sip of her orange juice, her legs swing from her barstool excitedly. "So, where are we going shopping?"

"Oh, I have a few ideas."

CHAPTER SEVEN

Wren

Turns out, when Oliver said he had a "few ideas," he meant some of the most expensive boutiques in the entire city. I feel completely out of place in a sea of high-quality fabrics, surrounded by three men who won't stop looking at me like I'm their favorite thing in the world.

At the first shop, I grab something comfortable that I can wear for the whole day—including underwear, since I mysteriously couldn't find mine this morning.

By the time we walk into the second shop, I'm not really sure what the point is. I already have plenty of clothes to get me through the weekend. But all three of them insist, drowning out my protests with kisses and laughs.

When Elliot hands me a pretty lilac dress, I swallow. It's just the type of thing I like to wear on hot summer days. But I usually get my dresses from the thrift store near my apartment.

And speaking of my apartment, I'm pretty sure this thing costs as much as my monthly rent, but I can't find a goddamned price tag on any of these clothes.

"So?" Elliot pushes me toward the dressing room.

"Christ," I mutter. "I don't know why I keep speaking my thoughts out loud around you."

69

He chuckles. "I think it's endearing. Now go try it on. I think it'll look nice on you."

"You think anything looks nice on her," Oliver chimes in, following closely behind us. He plops down next to Rhett, who's lounging on the red leather couch outside the dressing rooms.

Rhett laughs, and I realize Elliot is giving Oliver a death glare. But I disappear into the dressing room and close the curtains before I see what happens next.

I slide out of my new clothes, admiring the softness of the simple v-neck shirt I picked out. When I pull on the dress, I have to smile.

It *does* look nice.

Getting the zipper up is easy since it's on the side. I do a little twirl, watching myself in the mirror. It's the perfect type of dress for a summer picnic.

I imagine myself on a soft blanket in the middle of a park, surrounded by Elliot, Oliver, and Rhett. The thought makes me happy. But just as that warm feeling hits me, it turns cold.

"Don't you *dare* catch feelings, Wren Taylor," I whisper to myself, jabbing a finger at my reflection. I can't invest my emotions in these three men.

Even if it's just for a weekend.

Even if they all look at me like they want to keep me.

I just can't end up with a broken heart again.

I take a deep breath, and the tears building at the backs of my eyes dissipate. My hands run down my sides, and my fingers snag on something at my hips.

I gasp.

"Wren?" I hear Elliot say. "Are you okay?"

I turn, ripping the curtains open with a grin. *"It has pockets!"*

. . .

We stop for a quick lunch at a small diner. I expect us to head to my apartment next, but when we all pile into the SUV, Elliot takes us in the opposite direction.

"Are we going to *another* store? You three are wild."

Oliver is in the front seat, and he turns to give me a wink.

"Just so you're aware," Elliot says in a slightly annoyed voice, "this was *completely* Oliver's idea."

Rhett and I both give each other confused glances. I slide my hand onto his lap, and he only tenses for a moment before he covers it with his own.

When Elliot pulls into a parking spot a few minutes later, I only need to glance out at the storefront for a second before I burst into a fit of laughter.

Elliot seems relieved by my reaction, but Rhett still looks uneasy.

Oliver hops out of the car, opening my door and pulling me out. "I wanted to go here first, but *someone* insisted on getting you real clothes first." He sticks his tongue out at Elliot.

I can't help but giggle as we make our way inside. The boutique owner greets us, furrowing her brows at the sight of three men walking in with one woman, but I ignore the look.

"Oooh! I like this one." Oliver grabs a cute bodysuit from a rack. It's black, lacy, and—

"Of course you'd go for the boob-less one," Elliot mutters.

Both he and Rhett look a bit uncomfortable, while Oliver is like a kid in a candy store. Actually, that's not quite right. I think Rhett might be literally frozen in place by the door.

"Hey," I say, grabbing his hand and then Elliot's. "Why don't you two come with me." I lead them to the back, where the dressing rooms are. They're practically in their own room, probably for privacy's sake, which is nice. "You two stay here, and Oliver and I will do the shopping. But don't worry, you'll still get to see everything I try on."

Rhett lets out a giant breath, pulling me into his arms and kissing me with relief.

"Please don't force Wren to try on things she doesn't like," Elliot says to Oliver in a cautious voice.

Pressing a hand to his chest, Oliver tries to feign a hurt look. "I'd never!"

I raise an eyebrow. "Then put the boob-less one back."

His face falls. Rhett shoves him toward the front of the store, shaking his head, and Oliver listens without a second glance at me.

Turning to me, Elliot takes my hands in his. "If you get uncomfortable, or if you don't want to do this—"

I kiss him to shut him up. "Just sit. I'll be back soon."

When I head back out front alone, Oliver already has an armful of lacy, colorful lingerie sets.

"To be approved by you, of course. And I put the boob-less one back. I promise."

With a kiss on his cheek, I say, "I know. I trust you." And I mean it. Then, looking at everything he has in his hands already, I frown. "This is a lot for one weekend, Oliver."

His smile wavers, but only for a second. "Well, don't women like wearing sexy stuff even if no one sees it? For confidence or something like that?"

"Something like that." I pull a tiny silk robe from a rack, checking the size before tossing it onto Oliver's pile. He just grins.

Damn. He was dead serious when he said he wants to spoil me.

Fifteen minutes later, Oliver and I head to the back of the store, ignoring the blushing woman behind the checkout counter. Thankfully, no one else is here, so we have free rein of the place.

Elliot gives me a questioning look as Oliver brings everything into one of the dressing rooms. With a thumbs up, I head inside and shoo Oliver out.

It doesn't take long for me to pull on the first set, a tiny light blue thong and a matching bra that pushes my boobs up. But when I turn to look at myself in the mirror, my stomach turns.

Over the years, I've done a lot of work to come to appreciate and love my body. But a lot of that was trashed by the hateful comments Adam would make whenever I dared to show my body when I was bloated or after I ate.

I clench my fists. *Food in your stomach is normal, Wren. You're human. And humans fucking eat.*

But Adam's comments fill my mind, and tears fill my eyes.

They won't say those kinds of things to you.

They're different.

. . . But what if they're not?

"Wren?" Oliver's voice comes from the other side of the curtains, soft and concerned, and I realize I'm sniffling. "Are you okay?"

"Y-yeah." But I can't even say a single word without my voice breaking.

The curtains open, and Oliver steps inside before shutting them again. He frowns at my tears, and then at my arms hiding my stomach.

For a second, he looks angry. But then he takes a deep breath and tugs me closer to him. "Tell me what's going through your mind right now."

I shake my head, looking anywhere but him.

"Are you insecure? Did I get you the wrong size in something?"

I inhale a shuddering breath as more tears fall onto my cheeks. But I just can't make myself say it. It's too much, too intimate for a man I can't let myself get attached to.

For a moment, I wish he'd tell me he doesn't like my body, just so I can get out of this weekend. That way, my heart isn't at risk of getting trampled over at all.

"Stab in the dark," he says lowly, his fingers tracing over my arms that are still locked over my stomach. "You're insecure about how you look?"

With a sigh that I hope says, *I hate you for reading me so well,* I nod.

He pulls my arms away from my body. "The expectation of women to be stick thin is stupid, and it does more harm than good. You know that, right?"

"Yes," I mumble.

He kneels, holding my hips in his hands and kissing my stomach. "I like you like this. It means we're feeding you well. And I obviously like spoiling you." He grins up at me.

"I don't think I can do this," I whisper, wiping at my cheeks.

"You don't have to do anything you're not comfortable with, princess. Do you want to try everything on without showing us?" He kisses my stomach again, and it takes everything in me not to suck it in. I have a feeling he wouldn't like that.

I nod.

"Do you still want to spend the weekend with us?"

I hesitate, squeezing my eyes shut so I don't see the disappointment I just *know* is written all over his face.

"You can say no, Wren. But we're still buying you whatever you like from here and sending you home with all your clothes."

I sniffle, barely holding back a sob, and look at him. "I want to, Oliver. I do. But I'm scared. Really, *really* scared."

For a moment, he looks wounded. "That we'll hurt you?"

I shake my head. "That I'll hurt myself."

He stands, brushing my hair out of my face. "Unfortunately, I can't help you with that. But I would if I could."

I bury my face in his chest, inhaling his vanilla and woodsy scent. We stay like that for a minute or two before I look up at him. "I'll come back with you."

He grins.

"You're sure they won't mind that I'm not going to show what I try on?" My fingers fist his shirt.

"Positive. All of this isn't for us, princess. It's for you." After I give him a disbelieving look, he laughs. "Okay, it's *mostly* for you. But I can't lie. I'm excited to see what you pick out." He leans closer and murmurs in my ear, "And even more excited to tear it all off of you so we can use you like the pretty fucktoy you are."

His words send a shiver through me. Then I push him toward the curtains. "I'll be out soon. And thank you, Oliver."

He kisses me on the forehead, squeezes my hand, and then disappears.

I turn to the lacy pile of lingerie sitting in the corner of the dressing room and smile.

Told you. They're nothing like Adam.

CHAPTER EIGHT

Rhett

Seeing Wren's eyes red from crying sends a wave of fury through me that I'm barely able to get under control. I stand behind her while she checks out with Oliver, trying to calm my facial expressions. When the checkout lady gives me a frightened look, I figure I'm doing a shitty job.

Typical.

Turning away, I take a few deep breaths. Trace my fingers over the seams of my jeans and focus on the feeling of the rough fabric. Crack my knuckles.

Whoever dared to make her feel insecure about herself is going to pay—dearly. And I'm already pretty sure I know who it was.

I feel a soft hand wrap around mine. It sends a wave of calm through me that still feels foreign in my body. I kiss the top of Wren's head before giving her what I hope is a convincing smile.

"Ready?"

"Definitely."

I think lingerie is pretty, and Wren seems happy with what she picked out—after her breakdown in the dressing room, of course. But being in a lingerie store for an hour? Really not my thing.

Oliver adds the bags to the trunk, and we climb into the SUV again. This time, before Wren can reach for her seatbelt, I pull her into the middle seat and strap her in. I keep my arm around her, and she settles into my side with a sigh. She runs her hand up and down my thigh with soft strokes.

Two days. Technically, one and a half now. It's not enough fucking time to get her out of my system. Hell, I'm beginning to think I never will.

When Elliot pulls into the parking lot of Wren's apartment building, her hand freezes on my leg. Her gaze is locked onto a green sedan close to the entrance.

Wren's deep, relaxed breaths quickly turn to shallow, panicked ones. Her nails dig into my pants, although I don't think she realizes it.

Shit. I can barely handle my emotions, let alone someone else's. When I heard her crying in the dressing room earlier, it felt like I couldn't move. And now I'm the one in the backseat with her while she's about to break down again.

"Who?" I grunt out.

Wrong thing to fucking *say, Brooks.*

"Adam," she whispers. "My ex."

I hear Elliot undoing his seatbelt. "We're coming up with you."

She's about to protest, but she clamps her mouth shut at the look Elliot gives her in the rearview mirror. It's for the best. When Elliot's protective side comes out, it's smart to stay out of his fucking way.

We head up to her apartment, and I keep her tucked into my side.

In the elevator, she swears under her breath. "He has a key. I completely forgot."

"Any idea what he wants?" Elliot says without looking at her. Also for the best. I can feel the anger radiating off of him, and it makes me wonder what exactly he knows about this Adam guy that he hasn't told us.

"Probably just to talk." She's trying to keep her voice even, but she's not doing a great job at it.

When we get to her apartment, she turns to us. "If you guys don't mind, I'd like to try to talk to him alone. Just to see why he's here. I have a feeling he'd be pretty intimidated if I walked in with three guys behind me."

I grunt at the idea.

"I'll leave the door open," she says gently. "That way you can hear everything."

I hate it, but I nod. When she disappears into her apartment, it feels like she's carrying a part of my heart with her.

"Adam," I hear her say. "What—oh, god. What did you do?"

I clench my fists. The tension coming from Oliver and Elliot tells me they're struggling to stay put as well.

"You went home with someone last night," a male voice yells. "Ben was there. He told me. How could you do that?"

"That's rich coming from you," she snaps. "Get out, Adam. You've made enough of a mess."

"I've been calling you for days." His speech is slurred. Is he seriously *drunk?*

When I hear movement, I can't help it. I move closer, peeking through the crack in the open door. There's shit all over the floor, and he's standing a yard or two away from her.

If he takes one more goddamned step toward her . . .

"I don't have a particularly good reason to talk to you," she says flatly, looking around the apartment. It's a *mess.*

"Yes, you do!" he shouts. Then he grabs a mug from the kitchen counter. The way he's standing and glaring is all too familiar to me.

Fuck.

I barrel into the room just as he winds up for the throw. I grab Wren, pulling her back and behind me, but I'm not fast enough. The mug still catches her shoulder before crashing to the ground.

She lets out a shocked noise as I shove her behind me.

"Who the fuck is this?" Adam shouts. "Did you go home with him? Have you been sleeping with him behind my back the whole fucking time?"

Wren steps out from behind me, pushing my hand away when I try to force her back. *"You* cheated on me, Adam. Seriously, what's wrong with you?"

She turns when Elliot comes to stand beside her, and I can feel Oliver right behind us.

Adam's gaze settles on us, his eyes widening. "Babe, what's going on? Who the hell are these guys?"

I step forward. "Right now? Your worst *fucking* nightmare, buddy."

He takes a step back, tripping over a broken vase on the floor and falling on his ass. But I just grab the collar of his shirt and haul him back up.

"Who the fuck do you think you are, that you can speak to Wren like that?" I demand.

He sputters, but I barely notice. All I see is red. I need to get this guy out of here. If I lose it in front of Wren—

"Rhett." Elliot places a hand on my arm, and his gaze meets mine. "Not here."

I let out a string of curses, because he's right. Even if I get Adam outside, it's still too public of a place. Too many potential eyewitnesses. Too many security cameras.

With a grunt, I drag Adam out of the apartment. "Car keys." This kid is in no shape to drive, and he might not care, but I'm not letting him kill someone in a crash just because he got dumped.

Adam looks at me like I'm an idiot.

"Do you *want* to have the shit beat out of you?" I slam him against the wall. "Because I'm about to lose my fucking patience."

He lets out a terrified noise, fumbling in his jacket pocket before pulling them out. I snatch them from his hands. "You'd better watch your back, kid. Because you'll pay for hurting Wren." I shove him down the hallway so hard he stumbles and falls. "Get lost," I snap. "And don't *ever* call her babe again." I don't move, watching until he flees down the hallway and into an elevator.

When I step back into the apartment, Wren runs into my arms.

"Are you all right?" I pull away from her, tugging off her coat and pushing the sleeve of her shirt up. She winces when I touch her shoulder, and the simple movement solidifies my resolve.

Adam will pay. *Tonight.*

"I'll be fine," she says in a failed attempt at a cheerful tone. But her voice is shaking—along with her hands. "Thank you for pulling me out of the way. I think I was too stunned to move."

I pull her into a hug, pressing my lips to her hairline. He was aiming for her head. An image of Wren crumpled on the floor, bleeding, flashes through my mind, and I hold her tighter.

"Rhett," she wheezes, pushing against me.

Shit. I release her, and she gasps in a breath, clinging to my shirt. "Sorry," I mutter.

But she just shakes her head, giggling, before pressing her lips to mine. I let it ground me, deepening the kiss and cradling her face in my hands.

When she pulls away, it's with a contented smile. But it disappears the second her eyes leave mine.

It's then that I finally get a good look at her apartment. I was wrong earlier—it's not a mess. That implies a lack of cleaning. This place is *trashed*.

The cabinets in her kitchen are open and empty, most of the dishes smashed. The same thing is true of her bookshelf, and there are broken picture frames littering the floor.

"Oh no," she says softly, picking up an old book. Half the pages have been ripped out and are scattered over the ground. "I've had this copy since high school."

When I get a look at the spine, that uncontrollable anger comes back full-force. It's *A Tale of Two Cities*.

I'm going to rip that motherfucker to shreds.

"Where's your broom, Wren?" Oliver says.

She looks up, glancing between the three of us. Her eyes widen, and she shakes her head. "No, don't. It's my mess to clean up, and it'll take hours. I'm not destroying your weekend like this."

I almost tell her that sending us away is the thing that actually *would* destroy our weekend, but I hold my tongue.

Thankfully, Elliot steps in. He pulls her close, taking the book from her hands and kissing her nose. "It won't take that long with all four of us. Let us do this for you, love. And then let us take you home so we can help you forget that this ever happened."

Her eyes fill with tears, and he wipes them away as they fall. When she nods, the three of us let out a collective sigh of relief.

We get to work, Oliver with the broom and Elliot helping Wren put everything back on her bookshelf. I work on getting all the broken dishes off the counters, careful not to cut myself.

After fifteen minutes, the apartment is already looking much better. Except, I notice, now there's blood on the floor by the bookshelf. For a moment, I'm not sure where it's from, but then Wren steps into my view.

She's limping, and when she moves forward, she leaves a little pool of blood behind.

"Wren." I'm moving toward her before I even realize it, sweeping her into my arms. "Why did you take your shoes off, sweetheart? There's glass everywhere."

"What?" She tries to squirm out of my arms, but I nod to the floor. When she sees the blood, she frowns. "I didn't even realize I was bleeding." She raises her foot in the air, watching in surprise as blood trickles down her heel.

Both Elliot and Oliver turn at her words, but they get back to work when they see that I have her.

"Your foot was hurting you, and you didn't even—" I stop before I say something I'll regret. *Her ex just trashed her apartment. She's flustered and exhausted. Don't scold her.* "Let's just get you cleaned up."

I head down a narrow hallway, assuming the bathroom is at the end. But I only take a half-step in before freezing.

Adam wrecked it in here, too. But even worse than that is the red lipstick he smeared onto her mirror, writing out *stupid bich.*

The irony of the spelling error isn't lost on me.

"What?" Wren tries to get a peek, but I step outside.

"Ell," I say down the hallway, gesturing with my head to the bathroom.

He stalks inside, swearing under his breath when he sees the mirror.

"What?" Wren tries to wiggle free from my arms, but I clamp down on her. With a groan, she gives up, flopping dramatically and letting her head fall back.

"Do you have makeup wipes, love?" Elliot begins searching through all the shit that's scattered on the floor, careful not to step on anything.

"Yeah, they're on the shelf above the toilet. Well—they *should* be, anyway."

Elliot turns, scratching his head, before leaning down and snatching a package from the floor. "Found them."

He gets to work wiping at the mirrors. Wren glares impatiently at me, but I ignore her. I'm too focused on taking deep breaths and too scared that if I look at her, she'll think the anger strangling my entire body is directed at her.

Elliot steps back from the mirror with a nod. He passes us, giving Wren a quick kiss on her forehead before crossing the hall and switching on the light to the bedroom. As I set Wren on the bathroom counter, I glance inside.

It's as much of a wreck as the rest of the apartment, with pretty sundresses strewn everywhere, her lamp knocked over, and her laptop smashed to pieces on the floor.

God, that bastard.

"Is it bad?" She looks up at me, her impatience from earlier gone.

I take a look at her foot, gently wiping away the blood with some toilet paper. Breathing a sigh of relief, I say, "No. Just a cut. I don't think you even have a piece of glass stuck in there." I cut her a hard look. "Which means you're *lucky*. It could've been worse."

Her shoulders sag, and she looks down. "I'm sorry. I really don't know what I was thinking."

It's not your fault, I want to say. Because, really, it's mine. I never should've let her walk in here alone. If I hadn't, Adam wouldn't've thrown a mug at her, and she wouldn't be nearly as shaken.

Apparently, my thoughts are displayed right on my face, because Wren shakes her head. "Don't blame yourself, Rhett. He's never been violent like that before."

My heart stutters at her words. "Like that? What do you mean?"

She just shrugs, staring at my chest.

"Wren." My voice is harsh as I grab her chin, forcing her to look at me.

She stops breathing. One look in the mirror tells me that I've finally snapped. The anger that should be safely tucked away is on full display, and it's probably terrifying for her to see.

"Fuck," I mutter, releasing her. I place my hands on either side of her, bowing my head until it hits her shoulder. "Breathe, sweetheart."

She does, even if it's a bit shaky. "He just throws things when he's angry with me sometimes. But he's never aimed at me before. That's all." Her voice is small, almost afraid, and I hate that I'm the reason why.

"Did he scare you?"

I feel her nod.

"Then he shouldn't've fucking done it." I raise my head until I'm looking into her soft eyes. "I'm sorry, Wren. I shouldn't have been that harsh with you."

"You're not angry with me?" she whispers.

"God, no." I kiss her lightly. "I don't think I could ever be angry at you, sweetheart."

She lets out a sigh, wrapping her arms around my neck, and I let her hold me for a minute. Then, when my back can't take the awkward position any longer, I pull away.

It only takes a minute to clean and bandage her foot. We finish cleaning up, refusing to let Wren stay on her feet and almost tying her down to the couch when she won't listen. Then, once she's packed a bag, we head out.

On our way to the car, I snap a picture of the back of Adam's car and send it to a friend. I've already got one hellish night planned out for that asshole, and I can't wait to get started.

. . .

When we get back home, it's almost time to eat again. We order pizza at Wren's request, and then we all shower.

I drag her into my bathroom and take my time soaping her up. She does the same to me, giving every part of my body a kiss after she cleans it. It's weird being completely naked in front of someone other than Elliot or Oliver, but I shove the feeling aside and try to enjoy myself.

By the time we're done, I'm surprised we've both managed to control ourselves and not go at it in the shower.

While we dry off, she keeps looking like she wants to say something, but she doesn't. She changes into black, lacy panties and a matching bra that does wonders for her form.

"Are you trying to kill me?" I say, pushing her onto the bed. But I kneel down and take her foot in my hand, replacing her bandage.

She opens her mouth, but then she shuts it again.

"What?"

"Uhhh—nothing."

"Spit it out, sweetheart, or I'll force it out of you."

She squirms on the mattress, rubbing her thighs together. "Well, it's just that there's three of you." She says it like that should explain whatever it is she's thinking.

"And?"

She bites her lip. Takes a deep breath. Looks anywhere but me. Finally, with her eyes squeezed shut, she blurts, "I've never had anal sex before."

I give her an amused look. *That's* what has her so worked up? God, this woman. "Do you want to?"

"Maybe. Yes? I think so."

I nod, kissing her inner thighs. "That's not exactly something you just jump straight into. It takes some adjusting."

"I've done some training." She squirms again. "And I liked the way it felt. But Adam never wanted to . . ." She looks down at her hands. "You know."

I smirk. She's so fucking cute when she's flustered. "Stick it in there?"

She groans, covering her face with her hands. "Don't laugh."

"Oh, I'm not laughing." I grab her legs and pull her to the edge of the bed. "Lift your hips for me, sweetheart."

She does, and I slide her panties off, throwing them to the floor. Then I spread her legs and dive in.

"What are you doing?" she gasps, grabbing onto my hair.

"Getting you relaxed," I murmur into her. "And getting a better taste of you than what I got this morning."

She moans, falling back onto her elbows. It doesn't take her long before all she's saying is my name, over and over again, with increased intensity. Finally, when I suck her clit into my mouth, she cries out. She tries to buck her hips, but I keep them firmly pinned to the bed.

"How are you so good at this?" she whispers.

I don't answer, sliding into her as far as I can go. Then I move down to her other hole and circle it with my tongue. She jumps at the new sensation, moaning when I give her a lick.

When I stand, she watches me as I head over to my nightstand and pull something out. When I turn, her eyes are on the butt plug in my hand.

"You're going to wear this through dinner," I tell her. "And then while we fuck you senseless afterward."

She nods enthusiastically, sitting up.

"Get on your hands and knees."

She does, putting her ass on display for me. I grab some lube, using plenty of it to prep her with my fingers before I slide the plug into her a bit.

"Take deep breaths for me, sweetheart, and relax."

She obeys, moaning as the plug fills her. I let her adjust for a second, squeezing her ass cheeks.

"How does it feel?"

"Good," she whispers.

Perfect.

CHAPTER NINE

Wren

None of the guys can stop staring at me during dinner. I put on this set specifically to tease them, and also because I know there's no point in putting it on right before sex. Oliver has already *very* clearly expressed that he can't wait to rip it off of me.

Once we're done eating, I suggest a movie, knowing I'm too full to do anything except let my stomach settle. They all agree, and we move to the living room.

Elliot pulls me onto the love seat with him, and I sigh happily. I've been with him for most of the day, but I haven't had alone time with him like I have with Oliver and Rhett. So I snuggle up to him, pressing small kisses to his neck until he groans.

"You're going to be the death of me, love," he murmurs in my ear as the movie starts.

"Not for a long time, I hope." The words are out of my mouth before I can stop them. My body tenses, but he just kisses me like it's a perfectly normal thing for a weekend fling to say.

He holds me close, and I do the same, running my hand over his hair. I forget what I said, focusing on the movie and his calming heartbeat instead.

About halfway through, Oliver says, "I vote it's someone else's turn."

I giggle, and Elliot squeezes me before he lets me go. With a smirk, I head toward Oliver's chair, but at the last possible moment jump onto the couch next to Rhett.

Oliver's face turns serious. "You're going to pay for that later."

I just stick my tongue out at him before pressing a kiss to Rhett's cheek. He's tense, and he looks lost in thought. But when I kiss his lips, he moans, and I finally get all of his attention.

"God, I can't wait to fuck you," I say, the confidence and forwardness in my voice shocking me. But Rhett eats it up, sucking on my bottom lip.

"We'll see." Then he turns to continue watching the movie.

I moan, and Oliver snickers. He shoots me a glance that says, *If you'd come over here instead, I'd be fingering you already.*

Or at least I *think* that's what that look means. Either that, or, *I really want to fuck you right now.*

After about fifteen minutes, my hand drifts to Rhett's cock. He's already hard, and after a few strokes, he's rocking his hips into my hand. But then he reaches around me and unclasps my bra, yanking it off of me.

I squeal as he turns me around and lays me across his lap, so my breasts are on complete display for him. I hear Oliver moan, and then Elliot mutter a *"Fuck."*

Rhett pinches my nipples hard enough that I cry out. "Christ, that sound," he murmurs, and then he does it again.

My back arches as I yell out his name. He squeezes my breasts, smirking in satisfaction as I writhe under his hands. One of them slips between my legs, teasing me through the thin fabric of my panties.

"Do you want us, sweetheart?" he says, his voice thick with lust.

"Yes," I say on an exhale, moaning when his thumb brushes over one of my nipples.

"All three of us?"

"Yes, please."

"What does that make you, Wren?"

I gasp as his fingers slip into my panties. When he finds my clit, it's like a thousand tiny fireworks going off in my body.

"Answer me, sweetheart."

"Your dirty little whore," I say, and I hear Oliver groan.

"That's right." He pinches one of my nipples again, and my eyes roll into the back of my head.

"Who else are you a filthy whore for?" His finger circles my clit, and for a moment I forget how to think. "Who else, Wren?"

"No one," I whisper, and I think I might actually mean it.

"Good answer. Now suck my cock like the good girl you are."

I scramble onto my hands and knees on the cushion beside him. He slides his pants and underwear down his legs, and I moan at the sight of him. I got to taste him last night, but he was in control.

Tonight? I can take my sweet time.

I take his tip into my mouth, swirling my tongue, and he groans. He steadies me as I stroke him with one of my hands, slowly taking more of him in. And once he hits the back of my throat, I come up slowly, sucking hard.

"Jesus, Wren." Rhett grabs the hair at the base of my neck. "Do that again."

I do, listening as he swears under his breath. It might just be the hottest thing I've ever heard. As I'm repeating the action again, I feel hands dragging my panties down my legs. Oliver groans in front of me, so it must be Elliot.

I lick Rhett from his base to his tip, cupping his balls, as Elliot slides into me. "Oh god," I whisper, my lips brushing against Rhett's cock. I've never felt so *full* before, and it's an entirely different sensation.

"Did I tell you that you could stop?" Rhett forces my head down, and that action alone almost makes me come.

I focus on his tip, sucking and licking, before he takes control. His thrusts are punishing, but in the best way. I don't even mind when I gag, or when my tears fall onto his lap.

Elliot picks up his pace, and one of his hands snakes around my hips until his finger finds my clit. The added sensation is overwhelming, like my whole body is screaming for release.

"That's it, love," Elliot says. "You're taking us so well."

His words do me in, my moans muffled by Rhett fucking my mouth. The sound must push him over the edge, because I feel his cum coating my tongue.

When he's finished, he says, "Let me see." Rhett pulls my head up, grasping my jaw until I open my mouth. He looks his fill. "Swallow."

I do, licking my lips and panting.

"Oh, fuck," Elliot groans. His thrusts slow, and I relax into him while he comes. He stays inside me for a minute, and when I look back, he smirks, looking between me and the butt plug Rhett put inside me.

They've fucked any sense of embarrassment out of me, so I just hold his gaze.

When he pulls out of me, it's with a moan. I straighten, looking for Oliver, but Rhett grabs me.

"I'm not done with you yet." He kisses me before adjusting us so he's laying down and I'm straddling his face. "Sit."

My eyes widen. I've never done this before. "Like, *actually* sit, or—"

He yanks me down, and I let out a cry as he sucks on my too-sensitive clit. But his grasp on my hips is too strong, and I can't pull away.

"Rhett—Rhett, I'm too sensitive—oh *god.*"

Whatever he's doing with his tongue, it sends a shudder through my whole body. My hips rock against him involuntarily until he gives my ass a light slap.

"Oh fuck, Ell." The words come from Oliver, somewhere behind me.

I turn, watching as his eyes slide shut. With one hand, Elliot has his wrists pinned to the wall above him. With the other, he strokes Oliver's dick in torturously slow motions. They're both still mostly clothed, but it doesn't detract from how fucking *hot* it is.

Rhett slides his tongue into me, swirling it, before returning to my clit. Considering the moans coming from him, you'd think this is the first time he's ever tasted me—even though he just did mere hours ago.

As my orgasm builds, it gets harder to sit still. But every time I get close, Rhett pulls away, holding my hips when I try to find any type of friction. After he does it for the fourth goddamned time, I find myself begging for him to let me come.

He just lets out a dark chuckle. But he dives back in, this time letting me find my release. When I scream, he lightens the pressure on my clit but doesn't let up entirely. It draws out my orgasm in a way I've never felt before.

"Oh god, oh god, *oh god,* Rhett that feels—" I let out a long moan. The only thing holding me up right now is his hands on my waist. He scooches me down to his hips so he can sit up, and then he pulls me into his body while I try to remember my own name.

After a minute, I turn to watch Oliver. He's the only one I haven't had in my mouth yet, and watching Elliot stroke him makes me want him even more.

Rhett squeezes my ass. "Go on. Trust me, he wants you."

With a grateful kiss on his lips, I move to Oliver and Elliot, sinking to my knees. Oliver's eyes open when I place my hands on his legs, and he smiles down at me.

"It's about time you got over here so I can use you. Open up, princess."

Elliot releases Oliver's cock but keeps his wrists pinned above him. It doesn't stop Oliver from thrusting into me with such force he pushes me back a bit. So Elliot grabs the back of my head, holding me still, while Oliver hits the back of my throat.

"Such a good little slut," he says, panting. "I'm not gonna last long. You're going to take me down your throat. Understood?"

I give him a half-moan, half-gag as he pushes deep inside of me and holds himself there. When he pulls out, I barely have time to gasp in a breath before he does it again.

He lets out a deep groan, shuddering, and I swallow as he shoots spurts of hot cum down my throat. He swears, pumping into me one last time before pulling out.

"Jesus, that was amazing." He looks down at me proudly. "And you did so well. Did you like it?"

I wipe away the drool from my mouth, my gaze locked on his. "Yes."

"I know you did, princess. Now, what do you say?"

A small smile forms on my lips. "Thank you for fucking my mouth, Oliver."

CHAPTER TEN

Elliot

After we clean up, we settle back down to finish watching the movie. Wren is sandwiched in between Rhett and Oliver. And while I wish she was in my arms, I have to admit that the look on their faces sends a wave of happiness through me.

After a half hour, I look over to find Wren's sleeping body slumped into Rhett's. I expect to find her face peaceful, but instead a frown is etched into her beautiful features. She murmurs something that I can't hear over the movie.

My heart clenches as I remember Oliver mentioning that she had a nightmare last night and came barreling through the house to find him. Is she having another one right now?

As if to answer, she jumps awake with a yell. Rhett grabs her, immediately tense. She struggles against him, screaming, until she makes eye contact with me.

I don't remember standing or walking over to her, but here I am, my hand cupping her face. "You're safe, love. Do you remember where you are?"

She looks around, her eyes falling on Rhett, and then to the scratch marks on his arm. "Oh, Rhett, I'm so sorry. I didn't—" Tears fill her eyes as she takes his arm in her hands. "I forgot where I was for a minute."

He shakes his head, grabbing her face in his hands and planting a kiss on her forehead. "You were scared. Forget about it."

But the tears keep streaming down her face. "I don't want to hurt you. Any of you. I'm sorry, I—"

He places a finger over her lips, shushing her. His entire body is riddled with so much tension, I'm surprised he's even able to let out such a gentle sound. "It barely hurt, sweetheart. I've had a lot worse done to me."

Her eyes soften in sympathy, which causes him to pull back.

"What do you need, princess?" Oliver wraps an arm around her waist. "Something to drink?"

She nods. "Juice?"

"I'll get it," Rhett says gruffly, standing.

I crouch in front of her, taking her hands in mine. "A blanket? A distraction?"

"Both, please," she whispers.

While I grab her a blanket, Oliver pulls her onto his lap. "Tell me, what's your second favorite book? Elliot is gonna need a new one to read."

She bites her lip. "Probably *Pride and Prejudice.*"

Oliver rolls his eyes and pokes her side. "Do you read any books that *aren't* old?"

"I like fantasy."

"Any that we can make come true for you?" He winks, and I cringe.

"That was *terrible,* Oliver," she giggles. But her eyes drift down to his erection.

Well, at least I'm not the only one who can't control his dick around her.

"I'll take that as a yes. What do you want us to do?"

"Tie me up again?" She glances between us shyly.

"Oh, princess. With pleasure."

. . .

By the time Wren has finished her juice, she can't stop rubbing her thighs together. She hasn't let go of Rhett's hand since he came back. His tension from earlier is gone, and I can only hope it's because he used one of his breathing techniques instead of tacking something else onto his plans for Adam tonight.

Oliver whisks Wren off the couch, taking her to his room. I tie her legs to the foot of the bed while Rhett eats her out, and Oliver watches from the corner of the room.

When she comes, it's with a cry that goes straight to my dick.

I go next, kissing her body until she's begging for more. I bring her to orgasm quickly, leaving her trembling on the bed.

Then Oliver takes out her wand from his nightstand drawer.

Wren gasps. "That's—how—that's mine!"

With a smirk, he runs his fingers down her leg, stepping to the foot of the bed. "Found it while I was putting your room back together. Remember how I said you'd pay for teasing me earlier?"

Wren's eyes widen as she nods. "Oh no."

He grins. "You're so fucked, princess."

She tries to squirm away, but I've tied her too well. "What are you going to do to me?"

"Make you come until you beg me to stop." He turns the wand on, pressing it to her inner thigh. "Literally."

"Oh god," she whimpers. Then she yelps as he touches it to her clit. "Oliver, I'm still too sensitive, I—" She screams when he doesn't listen.

Her hips try to twist out of his reach, but she can only move a few inches. Rhett grabs her hands and pins them to the mattress above her head, watching her writhe.

Oliver removes the wand. She lets out a relieved sigh that's followed by a squeal when he touches it to her again. And this time, he doesn't let up.

"Oliver," she cries out. But she doesn't tell him to stop. Her eyes slide closed, and she arches her back. Rhett clamps a hand over her mouth when she screams, her hips bucking as she tries to find any relief from the sensation.

"Have you learned your lesson, princess?" He gives her a moment of relief before he goes back to torturing her.

"Please," she gasps. "I won't do it again. I—OLIVER!"

He chuckles. "Say the magic word, princess."

"Stop," she yells, finally collapsing when he pulls away. Her chest is heaving. "Oh my god. Oh my *god*."

Rhett kisses her gently, and I move to untie her.

"Tease me like that again, and I'll go longer."

Wren lets out a long moan. Her body is limp as we pull her up and into Rhett's lap. "I've never had anything like that done to me."

"First time for everything." Oliver kisses her forehead. "Now let's get you cleaned up."

She looks between the three of us, frowning. "But you guys didn't get to—"

Oliver presses his lips to hers. "Give your body a break, princess. Trust me, we got our fill."

. . .

The sound of the tub filling with steaming water gives me a minor distraction from my thoughts.

Rhett is set on his plan for Adam tonight, but I hate it. We never do anything this quickly. There's always extensive research and careful planning so we know what we're walking into.

Sure, we rarely deal with normal idiots like Adam. But that doesn't mean he's *not* a wild card.

I hear voices coming from the bedroom. The guys must be done with their shower with Wren.

"But I want to sleep with you, too," I hear her say.

"I know, sweetheart. But I can't tonight."

"You're working? Your jobs have really weird hours."

"No, not working. But I have something I have to do, and we don't want you alone in case you have another nightmare."

I walk in just as Rhett leans down to kiss her forehead. She's sitting on the bed, wrapped in the little silk robe she got earlier.

God, that was this afternoon? What a long day.

Worth it, I think as Wren smiles at me from across the room.

Rhett kisses her goodnight before turning to go. "I'll see you in the morning."

For a moment, I watch as he moves to leave. My mind is caught between *don't nag him* and *what if he never comes back?*

"Rhett," I call after him, jogging to catch up. I grab his arm right outside my bedroom. "Be careful. And *don't* go alone." My emotions come through in my voice more than I mean for them to.

I can't help it. Rhett can handle himself, but he's too angry to think straight right now. And if something happens to him, Oliver and I will never recover.

He pulls me in with a hand on the back of my neck and kisses me, soft and slow. When he pulls away, he smiles. "I'll come back in one piece. Promise."

It's a simple task—find Adam, give him a piece of *all* our minds, and come back. But as I watch Rhett walk down the hallway, I can't help the tightness in my chest. Letting him go feels like walking in a field with a hundred sniper rifles pointed at me.

Not safe, too vulnerable, and unable to do a goddamned thing to protect myself.

"Where's he going?" Wren asks, and I feel her arms wrap around my waist from behind.

"Don't worry about it. Now let's get you soaking."

We both strip, and I pull her into the tub, having her settle in between my legs like last night. But she twists, turning around so she's looking at me. Her eyes graze my chest, taking in the ink on my skin.

"I was too distracted to get a good look at you last night," she murmurs. Her fingers run over my body, lingering on my butterfly tattoo. "You all have this one."

I swallow. *Might as well tell her.* "Rhett had a sister. Significantly younger than him, by about ten years. When we were in high school, she was killed."

"That's terrible, Elliot. I'm so sorry." Her hand finds mine, intertwining our fingers and squeezing.

"She meant the world to all of us, but especially to him. When she died—it . . . gave us all issues. Rhett's always struggled the most. She was his little sister, after all."

"So the tattoo is to remember her by?"

I nod. It's more than that—a pledge to hunt down the people who killed her and make them pay. It was the decision that started everything.

But I can't tell Wren that. It's too much. And in twenty-four hours, she'll be gone. Back to being the barista we pine after every Friday.

Can we do that? See her every week but not touch her?

Fuck. We might have to find a different coffee shop. Part of me knows it won't matter—I'll never be able to scrub the feeling of having Wren close from my brain.

But one weekend fling can't turn into a relationship. There's no possible way she wants that, too. She's opened up to us a lot, sure. But she's still holding back. Why'd she do that if she wanted us?

It doesn't matter anyway. Letting Wren into our relationship would bring along too many complications and dangers. It wouldn't be fair to her.

Wren leans down, placing a kiss to the butterfly on my ribcage. Then she settles against me, her head on my chest.

"Comfortable?" I brush her hair to one side. "Are you sore?"

"Just a little," she says, yawning. Then she giggles. "I promise I won't fall asleep on you again."

My lips ghost across her hairline. "If you're tired, I don't mind. Let yourself."

I feel her tense. It's barely noticeable, but reading her body language has become like a second nature to me. I guess that's what happens when you can't take your eyes off someone.

"Why do you care about me so much?" she says softly.

"Who are you comparing me to?"

"What?"

"Who are you comparing me to? Because the real question isn't why I care so much. It's why the men who had you before me *didn't* care."

She lets out a breath. "I guess that's one way to look at it. All three of you are just so . . ." She shakes her head. "Never mind."

I don't press her. Whatever she was about to say, I have a feeling it's too much, too intimate. And that's the last thing we need right now.

We spend the rest of the bath in silence. I stroke her hair while she traces her fingers up and down my arm. It's nice. Comfortable.

In bed, she tilts her head and watches me. "You're worried. About Rhett?" There's a hint of fear in her eyes.

"Don't worry about it, love."

She bites her lip, her brows furrowing. After a moment, she scooches closer and wraps her arms around me.

And that's how we stay, until my eyes finally close and I drift off to sleep.

CHAPTER ELEVEN

Rhett

I don't want to bring Oliver with me.

Other than what a friend was able to dig up for me, this Adam guy is a mystery to us. He seems harmless, but I could be wrong. And I hate the thought of dragging Oliver into a situation without knowing what we're walking into.

But when I head downstairs, he's already waiting by the door, tucking his gun into the waistband of his jeans before shrugging on his coat.

I sigh. Maybe it's for the best. He won't sleep until I get back, anyway.

We climb into my truck, but I don't start it. There's something I've needed to say all day, but I haven't been able to get him alone.

When he sees my expression, he runs a hand over his face. "Please tell me you haven't been beating yourself up about this all day. You've been doing better, Rhett. It was just one slip-up."

Of course he's able to figure it out that quickly. When you've been with someone for over ten years, you learn them inside and out.

My knuckles ache as I grip the steering wheel too hard. "I don't want to have slip-ups. You both—all three of you—deserve better."

"Fuck," he mutters. Then he leans over the console and grabs my face in his hands. "You were trying to protect her, okay? I shouldn't've told her I'd be heartbroken if she decided not to stay. You were right to call me out on my bullshit."

Not by snapping at you, I almost yell. But that would defeat the purpose of this already-failed attempt at an apology. "I shouldn't've done it like that," I grit out. "And I'm sorry."

He touches his forehead to mine. "Apology accepted. I'm not holding it against you."

Part of the knot in my chest unravels, but my skin still feels vulnerable and prickly. I press my lips to his before turning on the truck and pulling out of the garage.

When I pull up a couple of blocks away from Adam's house, I let out a breath. *Almost there.*

"You good?" Oliver's hand covers mine over the gearshift.

I work my jaw. Tighten my fist and then unclench it. "Just don't let me kill him."

He nods, and we start moving. The snow crunches under our boots, and I keep my breaths even. When we get to his street, I pull on my gloves.

Just stick to your list. Hurt him enough that he'll never dare to touch anyone else again. And then get the fuck out.

His front door is locked, but I kick it down with ease, gun in hand. He's in the front room, sitting in an old armchair, an open bottle of whiskey next to him. One of his hands is clutching a gun that's pointed straight at my head.

"Get out," he yells, standing. "Or I'll shoot!"

Oliver swears behind me, and I hear the shot before it's even registered in my mind that he's jumped in front of me.

Panic seizes my chest until I see Adam stumble backward, clutching his arm. Blood soaks his sleeve.

Shit. The neighbors definitely heard that.

"Freddy's on tonight," Oliver says, watching as Adam's knees hit the floor. "There's no way he won't be the one who gets called to the scene."

"Good." That gives us more time.

Grabbing Adam's gun from the floor where he dropped it, I eject the magazine and check the chamber. Both empty. *What an idiot.*

"I'll watch the door," Oliver says, grimacing at it. My kicking it down completely ruined it *and* the doorjamb.

At least it was cathartic.

I grab Adam by his hair and drag him into the back of his house. The kitchen is tiled, so it'll be easier for whoever has to clean up the blood than the wooden floors of the front room.

I haul him up, tossing him onto the counter. Dirty dishes clatter, and I hear a few break, but I don't care. I rip off his belt, tying it around his arm. I didn't drive all the way over here just for him to pass out from blood loss.

"Please don't hurt me," Adam sobs. "I have a girlfriend. Her name is Wren. She won't be able to live without me, she'll be so—"

I punch him in his stupid mouth, and his head slams into a cabinet. "You really don't recognize me, do you?"

"No! I swear, I have no idea who you are or what you want. I'll do anything. Do you want money? Drugs? I've got both upstairs."

"I want you out of this city."

"Please, man. I can't leave. I've got family here."

"Don't care." I punch him again, my fist connecting with his jaw, and he slumps to the floor.

He lets out a pathetic groan as I hear the first sirens.

I crouch next to him, grabbing his chin and pulling his face to mine. "I've decided to go easy on you tonight. But if you're still here by the end of the week, I'll make your life a living nightmare."

"This is going easy?" he sputters. Blood is dripping from his mouth, and he coughs, spraying my face.

"You have no idea," I grit out. The things I could do to this punk—but I can't. Freddy's power is limited, and he can only help us get away with so much.

"I'll leave," he croaks. "Just don't hurt me anymore."

I release him, and his head hits the ground when he doesn't catch himself. With a disgusted glare, I kick him in the stomach once. And then again—for good measure.

I grab his keys from my pocket and throw them on the floor. I already wiped my prints off them and took Wren's key off the ring.

Adam groans. "How did you get these? Who the fuck are you?"

I ignore both of his questions. "Good luck finding your car. Heard it got towed. Can't remember where to, though."

With that, I head back out front. Freddy is just stepping inside, the lights of his car flashing red and blue from the street.

"We were never here," I tell him, and he nods. Then I grab Oliver, and we disappear out the back door.

. . .

When we get home, the kitchen light is on. The second I step through the garage door, I see Elliot sitting at the counter and Wren pacing the room in nothing but an oversized T-shirt.

She turns to me, and her eyes go wide. "Oh my god."

Guess I didn't get all the blood off my face.

For a moment, her feet are frozen to the floor, like she's holding herself back from something. Then she's running toward me, flinging her arms around my neck.

I grunt from the impact, wrapping my arms around her waist. "I'm okay, sweetheart."

"Wait, where's Oliver?!" she says in a panicked voice, pulling away and searching behind me. Her fingers grab onto my jacket, fisting the fabric tightly.

I look out into the dark garage. When I got out of the truck, he was on the phone with Freddy, explaining what really happened—even though the truth will never appear in the papers tomorrow.

He emerges from the darkness, grinning. "I'm fine, princess. Not even a scratch."

Wren relaxes into me.

"Why are you guys still up?" I inhale the sweet scent from her hair, and instantly my heart feels calmer.

"She's still Adam's emergency contact in his phone. Got a call saying he was on the way to the hospital, barely conscious." Elliot runs a hand over his face, trying to rub his tiredness away. "She put the pieces together pretty easily. Smart girl." He gives her a proud smile, which she returns.

"How did the authorities get called so quickly?" Elliot stands with a yawn.

"He had a gun pointed at Rhett. I shot him."

Elliot freezes. *"What?"*

Wren's arms tighten around me as she lets out a startled noise.

"It was empty," I say. "The stupid fuck probably didn't even know how to load it."

Elliot grips the counter. "Never again, Rhett. Next time, do the proper fucking recon."

I don't look at him. Can't. The terror in his voice is too much, and I know it's written all over his face, too.

"Please," he says, and I'm pretty sure his voice almost breaks.

I swallow. "Never again."

Wren shoves away from me. I feel empty without her against my chest, but I let her go. She glares up at me, and not in a playful way. My heart fucking stops when I see the tears in her eyes.

No. No, please, not you.

"If you would've asked, I could've told you he has a gun. *And* that he only got it to brag about it." She shoves her finger at my chest. "He doesn't know how to use it—although he *thinks* he does."

I just watch her, relief flooding my chest. *She doesn't hate me. It's the opposite. She cares too fucking much, just like I do.*

"Hey." Oliver steps forward, pulling her into his arms. "We're okay. He's safe."

"Barely," she murmurs, sniffling.

I reach for her hand, and she lets me hold it. God, she's shaking. But she pulls me closer, and I wrap my arms around both of them. In an instant, Elliot is on the other side of them, mirroring my movements. He leans his forehead against Oliver's with a relieved sigh.

But then Wren tenses, and her breaths turn shallow and panicked. We pull away, giving her some space.

"What if you go to prison?" she cries, looking between me and Oliver. Her tears finally spill over. "You can't go to prison!"

We all bust out laughing. Oh, she's *cute.*

"Not happening, princess. Don't worry about it."

She frowns, looking between the three of us. "What did you guys say you do for work again?"

"We didn't," I say firmly. "And it's staying that way. For now."

She huffs, but when Oliver kisses her, she pulls away with a tired smile.

"Yeah, you need sleep." Elliot scoops her up into his arms, and she laughs. "For real this time."

He kisses Oliver, and then me. Wren watches us with a soft expression on her face. Happiness? Contentment? Compersion? I can't quite place it.

She looks at me, stretching upward, and I press my lips to hers. Then, with a whispered, "Goodnight," from her, Elliot carries her upstairs.

I lean against the counter, closing my eyes. The entire drive home, I was able to listen to Oliver's voice as he made a series of phone calls. But now it's silent, and there's nothing to distract me from my thoughts.

What would've happened if Adam *had* known how to work that gun? If Oliver hadn't reacted so quickly? I'm not conceited, but I know what would happen to Oliver and Elliot if I got killed. And it wouldn't be pretty.

And now, Wren. She looks at me with the same amount of passion I feel toward her, but for some reason, she's holding back. It makes my chest feel weird.

I hear the sink turn on.

"C'mere. I'm getting that blood off your face." Oliver runs a paper towel under the water.

I move toward him, letting him scrub at my face until he's satisfied.

"Hand, too," he says, grabbing mine before I can tell him no.

He washes away the blood and cleans the cuts on my knuckles. I hiss when he pours rubbing alcohol over them.

"When was the last time you slept?" he asks without looking at me.

I've had terrible insomnia for years. It's helpful considering the weird hours we end up working, but I do tend to crash at the most inopportune times.

"I don't know." I rub my face with my free hand. "Wednesday night? Thursday morning?" *Tuesday afternoon. And only for a couple of hours.*

"You need to sleep."

"Not tired."

"Well, you're laying down with me. Because I don't want to be alone tonight."

Translation: I panicked when I saw a gun pointed at your head, and I need you close to me.

I nod. He and Elliot are my rock. Have been for years. So when I get a chance to be there for them, I refuse to let them down. Forget that being vulnerable with someone makes my skin prickle and my stomach turn. They're the two most important people in my life, and I'd do anything for them.

"Whatever you need, O. Whatever you need."

CHAPTER TWELVE

Oliver

In the morning, I wake to find Rhett still in bed with me. He's reading a book silently, unaware that I've opened my eyes.

I watch him for a moment. His brows are furrowed in concentration—he's probably reading some stupid nonfiction book—but other than that, he's completely relaxed. And while I doubt he slept a wink, at least he's getting some type of rest.

He glances over at me and smiles. "Morning."

I let out a groan, still too tired to figure out how to use words.

"I haven't heard Elliot and Wren get up yet. You want coffee?"

I nod, reaching out and resting my hand on his leg. *He's here. He's safe. No bullet holes present.*

"I'll go get some started."

"Okay," I croak out, rubbing my eyes.

However much I want him to stay and hold me until I wake up all the way, I don't ask. He's been sitting up in bed all night. The man is probably so restless he feels like he's about to burst.

Before he steps out of the room, I sit up. "Rhett."

He turns.

"Thank you. For staying."

A faint smile graces his lips, and then he's gone.

I grab my phone and scroll through my notifications until my eyelids don't feel like they weigh fifteen pounds each. After getting ready for the day, I head down to the kitchen.

Rhett hands me a cup of coffee with a kiss, and I settle onto a barstool at the counter. He can't stop doing things with his hands—fiddling with his own cup of coffee, opening and closing a drawer absentmindedly, pulling at his shirt.

How he has spare energy, I'll never understand.

"I think I'm gonna go on a run."

I frown. "In the snow?"

"The road's plowed fine. I've just been restless all night." He winces. "Not that I minded. I promise I didn't."

"I know," I say softly, sipping my coffee. "Do whatever you need. Just bring a weapon, please."

"Always." With that, he disappears, leaving his coffee abandoned on the counter.

With a sigh, I head to the sunroom. I drink my coffee, looking over the front yard. My gaze snags on Rhett, and I watch him walk down the driveway.

He'll be fine. He always is.

"There you are." Wren's sweet voice fills my whole body with warmth.

She's still in Elliot's T-shirt, but this time she's wearing panties. Unfortunately, I didn't have a chance to steal the ones she packed with her, or the ones we bought for her.

Regrettable.

"Missed me so much you just had to come find me?" I hold out my arm to her, and she settles into my lap.

We both watch Rhett together as he breaks into a jog. "Is he okay?"

My heart aches. "He hasn't been okay in a long time, princess. But he's . . . getting better."

Frowning, she runs a hand over my hair. "And you? After last night?"

I swallow and look away. There's a time and a place to open up to someone. Even then, it has to be the *right* person. And while I can't help but think that Wren might be that right person, it's definitely at a terribly wrong time.

Maybe if we didn't live lives that could potentially put her in danger.

Maybe if she didn't keep looking at us like she's afraid we're going to break her heart.

Maybe if we could guarantee that we could keep her safe—physically and emotionally.

But those are all just wishes. Dreams. The reality is that, at the end of the night, we're going to have to let her go—even though none of us want to.

She tilts her head, watching me, and I wonder what's going on in her head. What does *she* want? What fears are holding her back?

It doesn't matter. It wouldn't work, anyway.

"Oliver?"

Right. She asked me a question.

"I'll be fine, princess. We made it back safe, and your ex got what he deserved. Now, what do you want for breakfast? Eggs? Cereal? Waffles?"

She perks up. "Waffles, please."

"Then waffles you shall get."

CHAPTER THIRTEEN

Wren

We spend the day just existing together.

None of them will do more than kiss me, saying they don't want to make me too sore. It's sweet, but every goddamned thing they do turns me on, so it leaves me squirming with want.

Elliot wakes up some time before lunch, and we spend our afternoon hanging out in the living room—reading, playing games, completely *normal* stuff.

The whole day is a blissful masquerade of pretending that we're more to each other than we are. Pretending that, at the end of the day, I'm not leaving.

The thought makes my heart ache. I tried so hard not to let these men burrow their way into my affections, but I failed. I've never felt so *cared for* before, and I don't want to let it go.

But you barely know them, I tell myself all day. *Is it worth the risk?*

My heart tells me it is—that it'll be worth getting broken again if it means more time in the arms of Elliot, Oliver, and Rhett. But my mind isn't so sure, and it's always been more reliable than my foolish heart.

They've known each other since high school. And while they may be a few years older than I am, that's still almost ten years for *me.* So for them, it's even longer.

How can I compare to that? They know each other inside out. Could I fit into their relationship? Do they want me to?

As I'm sitting on the couch next to Elliot, the thought that they *don't* want me stings. Of course, this all started as a one-night thing with Elliot, and then it turned into a weekend.

But none of them have brought up the idea of extending this—for a week, a month, indefinitely, whatever.

And I'm too scared to brave asking the question myself.

"Something's on your mind." Elliot closes his book, setting it on the arm of the couch and turning to me.

Both Rhett and Oliver look up from the puzzle they're working on together. With all three of them watching me, I can't help but squirm.

"I don't really want to talk about it. If that's okay." I stare down at my book while I say the last part.

"Of course it is, love." Elliot kisses my forehead, and it sends a mixture of happiness and dread through me.

Maybe I should just leave now. The longer I draw it out, the harder this is going to be.

But I can't seem to bring myself to ask one of them to take me home. And when dinnertime rolls around again, I find myself sneaking into Elliot's room to change into the skimpiest, laciest nightgown I've ever seen.

It doesn't even come halfway down my ass, and it shows off a bit of underboob—which I'm sure will have Oliver drooling. With a smile at myself in the mirror, I turn, admiring myself from every angle.

Last night, it was ridiculously satisfying to watch all three men adjust themselves in their pants when I came down to dinner dressed in almost nothing. I can't wait to do it again.

I catch Rhett's reflection in the mirror. He's holding something in his hands that I can't quite make out.

"Christ," he mutters.

I turn, letting him admire my curves. "What do you think?"

"If I didn't know better, I'd say you hate us. You're really going to make us sit through dinner with you wearing this?"

I nod, giggling.

He sighs. "At least it'll be worth it." With a few steps, he's on me, backing me into the bed. One of his hands fists the hair at the back of my head, pulling it so I'm looking up at him. "Tonight, I'm taking this perfect ass of yours. And you're going to thank me afterward."

I nod, a smile forming on my lips.

"Now turn around and put your ass in the air."

I obey, gasping when he shoves my panties down and gives me a lick from my clit to my asshole.

"Relax, sweetheart."

I do, taking a couple of deep breaths. I feel his finger prodding me, already wet with lube, and I moan when he pushes inside of me.

"Tell me, do you want me?" He nips at one of my ass cheeks.

"Yes," I whimper as he adds a second finger. I haven't forgotten that he's only been in my mouth so far. "Please, Rhett. Please."

He eases his fingers out of me before replacing them with something else that's bigger, but not warm enough to be his cock. "You'll have to wait until after dinner."

I relax as he pushes the butt plug into me. Then he stands up, keeping a hand on my back as he admires his handiwork.

"You're going to feel so good, sweetheart. Now come and eat."

Downstairs, Oliver lets out a groan when he sees me. "What did I tell you about teasing me, princess?"

I just grin at him.

"We ordered takeout," Elliot says, pulling me into his lap. He's sitting at the table, picking at a bowl of grapes. My stomach growls at the sight, so he grabs one and places it against my lips.

I open my mouth. He slides it in slowly, and then he runs his thumb across my bottom lip. The simple action sends sparks shooting down my body. When the sweetness of the grape bursts on my tongue, I moan.

He gives me another one, and this time, I capture his finger in my mouth, too, sucking while he slowly pulls it out.

"You know what?" Elliot says, one of his hands running up my stomach before cupping my breast. "Fuck waiting until after dinner."

I roll my eyes. "You can wait."

"I don't think I can." He kisses the back of my neck. "You smell so fucking good."

His words cause me to shiver, but I don't give in. I tested my limits with Oliver last night. Today, it's time to see what Elliot will do when I tease him.

So I turn to him, wrap my arms around his neck, and lean in slowly for a kiss. But at the last second, I jump from his lap and bolt out of the room.

It's less than five seconds before he grabs me and throws me over his shoulder. I squeal, giggling as he hauls me back into the kitchen.

"You fuck us a couple times, and all your shyness disappears, huh? Trust me, love, it's in your best interest to drop the attitude right fucking now."

"Hmm." I tap my finger to my chin, like I'm thinking, which causes Oliver to snort. "Why don't you make me?"

He sets me down roughly, but it doesn't go unnoticed how he keeps his hands on me until I've gained my balance. "Get on your knees."

I raise an eyebrow. *"Make me."*

And oh, he does. With his hands on my shoulders, he forces me down until I'm at eye-level with the erection straining against his pants. He has it out in seconds, brushing the tip against my lips.

"Open up," he says, "so I can fuck the attitude right out of this pretty little mouth of yours."

For a moment, I just smile up at him. But the want stirring between my legs doesn't let me hold out for any longer. I flick my tongue out and lick him before opening my mouth wide.

"Good girl." He fists my hair, yanking me forward until his cock hits the back of my throat.

I gag, but I close my lips around him as he sets his pace—fast and punishing. All I can do is hold on to his legs and try to breathe. He groans when he looks down to see tears streaming down my cheeks and a mixture of saliva and precum trailing from my mouth.

"That's it. You're doing so well. Such a pretty little slut."

I whimper as he takes me even harder, his grip on my hair tightening.

"Tap my thigh if you need a break, love."

I don't. I've loved every gentle, caring thing these men have done for me. But this? I've wanted it for so long. I just didn't trust anyone to respect my boundaries the way they do.

"I'm going to come in your mouth," Elliot grunts. "But you're not allowed to swallow until I give you permission. Understood?"

I let out a strangled sound that I hope he takes as a *yes*. And then he swears, and his pace finally slows as I feel him finish in my mouth.

When he pulls out, I keep my mouth open so he can see, tilting my head back.

He smiles down at me. "I like you best when you look like this."

Then he walks behind me, and I hear him doing something, but I'm not quite sure what. Until I feel his hands on the back of my thighs, pushing them apart. And then he appears in between my legs, on his back and looking up at me.

"Sit."

I do, and his tongue lashes out at me, like he's still angry that I talked back to him. My moans come out garbled and muffled, since my mouth is still full of his cum. It's an odd sensation, and yet another thing I've never done before.

Elliot's hands come to my hips, steadying me, and I realize I've been rocking against his face.

"Sit still, or I won't let you come."

I whimper, my hands grasping his. Then he goes back to work, sucking my clit into his mouth.

Oliver kneels in front of me, his lips brushing across the skin of my jawbone. When he runs the pads of his thumbs over my nipples, and then pinches them between his fingers, it takes everything in my willpower not to scream.

"Fuck," he mutters. "You're so goddamned hot like this."

Then he leans down and sucks one of my nipples into his mouth. His tongue flicks it back and forth, and it sends the first wave of my undoing through me.

All I can do is keep my mouth clamped shut as my orgasm rips through me. Oliver catches me when I fall forward, and Elliot gives me one last lick before sliding out from underneath me.

He comes around to stand over me. "Show me one last time."

I open my mouth, panting.

"Swallow."

I do. I swear, I've never *wanted* to obey a man before these three. But now, I'm ready to do whatever the hell any of them tell me to.

"Such a good girl," Oliver says before pressing his lips to mine in a kiss that takes my breath away. "Mmm. Ell, you taste good on her."

Oliver pulls me up, and Rhett comes behind me. At some point, they both stripped. I take a deep breath to calm the butterflies that appear in my stomach at the sight of them.

"Are you ready for more, princess?"

I nod.

Rhett comes behind me, palming my ass. "Bend over, sweetheart, and relax."

Oh god.

I do, and he slowly pulls the butt plug out of me. He disappears for a moment, coming back with a bottle of lube in his hands and a smirk on his face.

Oliver bites my ear lightly. "We're both going to fill you, and you're going to take it like the good little slut you are."

"Oh, fuck," I whisper as Oliver picks up one of my legs, holding it to give them more room. I help guide his cock to my entrance, and we both moan when he slips inside.

Once he's settled into a decent pace, I feel Rhett fill me from behind. He's gentle, easing into me slowly.

My head falls back and hits his chest.

"Relax, sweetheart," he whispers in my ear.

Oliver slows, giving me a chance to catch my breath. Rhett pushes himself in further, holding onto my hips.

"You're doing so well, Wren." I don't know who says it—I'm too lost in the new sensations, in the way they both feel inside me.

My eyes meet Elliot's, and I find him watching with an appreciative look on his face. But I only catch his gaze for a moment before my eyes close from pure bliss.

"Oh fuck," I whisper, grabbing onto Oliver's shoulders.

He chuckles. "I don't think she's going to last long." As if to prove his point, his free hand snakes down my front, and he presses his thumb against my clit.

Tiny explosions erupt with every movement he makes. Rhett keeps his pace slow and steady, but Oliver's thrusts turn rougher as they push me closer to the edge.

One of Rhett's hands wraps around my throat, squeezing lightly. And then I'm coming, lost between the two of them. Rhett's other hand clamps over my mouth as I scream, and it only makes me come harder.

They don't relent—not until my body calms down, just to be manipulated into another earth-shattering orgasm. When they both finally come, my legs are shaking, and their arms are the only things keeping me from collapsing onto the floor in a shivering puddle.

Someone takes me into the shower, cleaning the sweat off my body. The faint smell of sandalwood and sweet citrus calms me as he dries me off.

And then my body is swinging, a pair of strong arms lifting me off the floor and carrying me.

Dread pangs in my heart, and I can't get rid of the nagging feeling that there's something I need to do. But I'm too sated and dazed to figure it out, so I drift off to sleep, sandwiched between two warm bodies.

. . .

When I wake, it's dark out. I'm on a couch, my head resting on some-one's leg. Flames flicker in the fireplace, the only light in the room.

"She needs to go," someone says. Elliot, I think.

"I don't want her to." Oliver's voice is pouty, and it puts a small smile on my lips.

"I'm pretty sure she works Mondays. She's gonna have to get home so she can get ready for work in the morning."

Are they talking about me?

"Why?" Oliver says too loudly, almost angrily. "Why can't we figure out a way to make this work? She means something to all of us, so why not just admit it to her? We can take care of her."

"That's way too fast, O," Rhett says from above me. His hand comes down to stroke my hair, and I have to fight the urge to look up at him. I want to hear where this conversation is going.

Elliot sighs. "Ol, you literally said *just Friday* that it's a bad idea to pursue a relationship with her."

"Well, I changed my fucking mind. I can't go back to just seeing her once a week. And neither of you can, either."

Oh my god, they're talking about me.

"I've been contemplating finding a new coffee shop," Elliot says in a defeated voice. He sounds . . . deflated.

"You're never going to get her out of your head, Ell. You said so yourself. We've wanted her for so long, and we never thought we could have her, but now she's *here*. How can you let her go?"

My heart squeezes. Are they really so head-over-heels for me that the thought of seeing me without having me would be that hard? Hard enough to make them switch coffee shops?

Wait. Why do they think they can't have me?

"What about what Wren wants?" Rhett's hand moves to my shoulder, running down my arm. "What if she wants us, too?"

I do. Fuck being careful.

"What if she doesn't? Besides, we all know it'd be too complicated. Our sleep schedules are a mess, and it's not like we can change that. And what about—"

"I know," Oliver snaps, and I can just barely see him slump in his chair in my peripheral vision.

"We need to take her home, and then we need to leave her alone," Elliot says. "This weekend has been amazing—a fantasy come true. But that's all it's been. A *fantasy*. We need to let her go and try to forget about her."

No, I shout in my head. But the sound echoes throughout the room, very real and *very* audible.

"Fuck," Rhett mutters, pulling me up and into his lap. "How much of that did you hear?"

Tears spring to my eyes, but I blink them back. This is *exactly* what I was afraid of. I caught fucking feelings, and they're going to do their best to forget me regardless of what I want. What *they* want.

I try to slide off his lap, but he holds me to him.

"What all did you hear, sweetheart?"

I turn to Elliot, and his face falls at my hurt expression. Yesterday, he made the claim that he cared about me more than any of the men who came before him. And I agreed with him. But now? Now, he just wants to forget me.

"Why?"

He sighs. "It's . . . complicated, love."

"Don't call me that."

He winces.

This was a mistake. This was a huge, giant mistake, and it's going to make your life so much more fucking miserable.

"I want to go home."

"Absolutely not."

I think we're all surprised when the words spill from Elliot's lips. I try to squirm from Rhett's arms, but he just holds onto me tighter.

"Not like this." Elliot stands, coming to crouch in front of me. "I need you to understand, Wren. It's not because I don't want you. We all do. But our lives are . . . different from other people's. It's not easy, and it's not always safe."

As he explains, I remember how they've all avoided telling me what they do for a living. Are they spies? Assassins or something?

"I don't understand," I say flatly.

He rubs his face with his hands. "I guess I'm worried we'd add more stress to your life than happiness, lov- Wren."

"But you won't know unless you try," I whisper. My tears have come back, and one falls onto my cheek.

He brushes it away tenderly, shaking his head. "I don't think it's worth the risk. You don't know what you're walking into."

Then explain it to me, I want to yell.

Is this weekend the universe playing some cruel joke on me? Breaking my heart, showing me that there *are* kind men out there, and then ripping them from my grasp?

No. *No.*

I can't watch myself fall apart again. I don't care if it's only been a weekend. Somehow these men have stolen my heart, in a much bigger capacity than I was prepared for.

And I can't just walk away.

I twist, looking at Rhett. "Let me go." When he hesitates, I brush my fingers across his cheek. "I won't run."

He swallows, his gaze piercing me, like he's looking straight into my heart. And then he releases me with a sigh.

Elliot touches my arm. "Wren, I think you should—"

"No!" I shout, standing and glaring up at him. "No. You don't get to be patient and gentle and fucking *nice* to me, just to do this. You don't get to make me feel the most cared for, the most safe, the most valued I've ever felt in my life, just to rip it away from me because you're afraid. I'm afraid, too, Elliot. Of *this*. Of getting my heart broken again. But the three of you have embedded yourselves so deeply into me that I don't think I'll ever get you out, so here I am. I'm fucking facing my fears, Elliot. So why can't you?"

He just stares at me for a moment. Oliver's mouth is hanging open, and while I can't see Rhett, I can feel his stare burning the skin on the back of my neck.

"Wren—"

"Don't you dare tell me I should leave," I whisper. Another tear falls.

He swallows. Sighs. "I think you're right."

I was already preparing a counter-argument, so his words are the last thing I expected. I stumble backward, shocked. Rhett places a hand on my back to steady me.

He thinks I'm . . . *right?*

"Jesus," Oliver mutters. "You can reason with this fuckwit? Shit. Now we're never letting you go."

CHAPTER FOURTEEN

Rhett

"You're an idiot, you know that?"

Elliot lets out an unamused laugh. "I don't think I'll ever forget."

We're both standing off to the side of the kitchen, giving Oliver and Wren a little privacy while they say goodbye. She decided she wants to spend the night at her apartment since she has to get up so early, and I volunteered to drive her home since my vehicle handles snow the best.

The thought of leaving Wren at her apartment for the night is like a punch in the gut. We've only had her for two days, but they've been so fucking perfect. I've always had Oliver and Elliot, and I always will. But none of us can deny how easily she fits in with us—like she was made for us.

When Oliver finally pulls away from Wren with one last kiss, I shove Elliot forward.

"Make it fucking count."

As Oliver moves to stand next to me, Elliot stays frozen, staring at Wren. She gives him a watery smile, and only when she holds out her arms to him does he step into her reach.

I don't know what they're saying to each other, but based on the look of relieved adoration on Wren's face, they'll be okay—with time.

And we'll make sure we have it.

A chance—that's what we all agreed to. It's too early to jump into any type of commitment until she gets to know us better, and vice versa. But all of us are determined to make this work, Elliot especially.

He just needed Wren to set him straight first.

Oliver checks his phone, sighing. "You shouldn't have any trouble tonight. But at the first sign—"

"How about this?" I kiss him on the forehead. "I'll call once Wren is in her apartment, regardless. And you don't leave Elliot alone to his thoughts. Pretty sure he's feeling like shit right now."

He nods, and I squeeze his shoulder. "I'll see you soon."

Wren finally lets Elliot go, and I let out a relieved breath at the lack of tears in her eyes. If she ends up crying on the way home, I'm not sure what I'll do. The best I really *can* do is hold her hand and try not to panic.

Shouldering Wren's bag, I grab Elliot before he walks away. He avoids my gaze, but I guide his chin up with two fingers. Yup—definitely feeling guilty.

I leave him with a kiss and a murmured, "Let it go." Then, with Wren's hand in mine, we head out to the garage. She holds on until the last possible second before climbing into my truck.

"Thank you for taking me home," she says as we pull out.

I just give her a smile, reaching over and putting my hand on her leg. With a happy sigh, she settles back, and we stay like that for the whole ride.

When I pull into her apartment building's parking lot, Adam's car is absent, as I ensured it would be yesterday afternoon. Still, I walk her up and check the place, just to be safe. Only then does she let out a relieved sigh.

But the tension in her shoulders returns a mere second later. Her gaze snags on a small table by the door. "Oh no," she murmurs.

"What?"

"He broke my vase. It was my grandmother's." Tears form in her eyes. "She gave it to me as a graduation present. Adam *knew* how much it meant to me." She looks to her torn-apart copy of *A Tale of Two Cities*. "Those are the things he seemed to have gone for first."

I already felt like the beating I gave Adam wasn't enough. Now? I told him to leave, but I might just hunt him down anyway.

Wren sniffles, wiping at her cheeks. "It's just so heartless. He's hurt me enough already. Why this?" She gestures to the empty table. "That vase was all I had left of her."

Stepping forward, I cup her face in my hands. I have no clue what to say. So I just wipe away her tears with my thumbs and press a kiss to her forehead.

Her face finally crumples, and she lets out a sob, burying herself in my coat. I put my arms around her and try to keep myself from tensing too much.

But that prickly feeling spreads like wildfire over my skin, and I have to focus on the snow falling outside the windows just to keep myself from shoving her away from me.

She needs this. It's just emotions. You can handle it.

So I hold her tightly, watching the snow and taking deep, even breaths. Her sobs calm after a few minutes, but her grip on me doesn't loosen.

"I can't get hurt again," she says eventually, her words slightly muffled by my coat. "Please. I don't think I can take it."

I stroke her hair. "We don't want to hurt you, Wren. I promise that's the last thing we'd ever want."

She nods, sniffling, before relaxing into my chest. She feels so small against me, yet she fits so perfectly. Then, with a sigh, she says, "I'm sorry for crying again. I promise I normally don't do it this often."

You can cry all the time.

Wait, no. Whenever you want to. Need to?

Fuck.

I cup her chin in my hand, and she looks up at me with tear-stained cheeks. With another deep breath, I try to think of all the things I want to say, but I can't figure out the best way to get everything out.

Fuck it.

"I know I'm not the best when it comes to affection, or a lot of emotions. But I want to be a safe person for you. I know this is all overwhelmingly fast for you, but I want to make this work. And last. So please—if I'm ever *not* giving you what you need from me, just tell me. I'll do anything to keep you, Wren. Including holding you while you cry, however often that ends up being."

She doesn't say anything for a minute. Just looks at me. It feels like my throat is caving in on itself. So I focus on the fact that she's still in my arms. Still holding onto me. Whatever I said couldn't've been *that* bad if she still wants to touch me.

"That might be the nicest thing someone's ever said to me," she whispers. Then she stands on her tiptoes and kisses me softly.

Relief floods me. "I meant every word," I say against her lips before deepening the kiss. I eat up her moans, sliding my tongue into her mouth. And then she's tugging my coat off, and I'm letting her, because goddammit, I don't want to leave.

Her hands come up underneath my shirt, hitting a hyper-sensitive spot, and I grab her wrists with a hiss.

She lights up. "You're ticklish?! Oh my god, yes!"

"Don't you *dare*."

Somehow, she squirms out of my grasp, tickling my sides. I buckle over, hugging my stomach to protect myself. She's giggling, trying to get to my armpits before she finally decides to go for the backs of my knees.

Once she's bent over, I grab her and throw her over my shoulder. "You're in deep trouble now, sweetheart."

She just laughs, contorting herself to tickle my armpits. I almost drop her halfway down the hall, but somehow I manage to control myself until we get to her bedroom.

"You think you can do something like that without paying?" I say, throwing her onto the mattress.

Wren bounces, grinning, before scrambling to the far side.

"Oh, so *now* you run." I grab her leg and pull her back to me. "Your choice, sweetheart. Either I spank your sweet ass until it's the only thing you'll feel when you sit down tomorrow, or I fuck you until I finish without letting you come." I undo her pants and pull them down her legs. "*Or* I can tickle you until you can barely breathe."

"Noooooo!"

"Then choose, before I choose for you."

She gasps when I yank her shirt over her head. Then she narrows her eyes, thinking, before saying, "How many spankings, exactly?"

"I'll go easy on you—*this time*—and say ten."

"Ten spankings, or I don't get to come."

"Correct."

She grins. "But if I choose spankings, you still fuck me?"

"Oh, it's definitely happening."

"*And* you'll let me come?"

"Maybe."

She bites her lip. Tilts her head. Unclasps her bra and throws it to the side. "Spankings it is. But if it hurts too much—"

"Then just say the word." I give her a gentle kiss, and she moans. Then I throw her onto her stomach, pulling up her hips so her ass is ready for me. I slide her panties down her legs and leave them gathered at her knees, taking in the view.

She looks back at me, curiosity shining in her eyes.

"You felt so good earlier." I watch as she smiles back at me, and then I wipe it off her face with a hard *smack.*

She yelps, and before she can recover I hit the same spot again. I massage her skin for a few seconds before moving to her other ass cheek, spanking the same spot on the other side twice.

When I look, I find her soaked and ready for me. "Are you going to tickle me again, sweetheart?" *Smack.*

"I mean, probably. It was funny."

Smack. Smack.

"Owwww!"

"Do it again, and I won't go so easy on you." I see the beginnings of a giant grin before she hides her face in her covers. I hit her again and she moans. "Do you like a little bit of pain with your pleasure, sweetheart?" *Smack.*

She squirms, gripping her comforter as I land the last hit. Then I step back, admiring the way she's still sticking her ass up in the air.

"You took that so well." I lean down, giving her clit a single lick before pulling my shirt over my head. "Come here."

She crawls over to me, and her lips part as I finish stripping. Her eyes travel downward. When I grab her by the back of her head and yank her up, she gasps.

With my face mere inches from hers, I say, "What are you?"

I watch as her pupils dilate. "Your personal fucktoy."

"That's right." I kiss her roughly, and she moans. "Tonight, I fucking own you. And I'm going to make sure you feel it all day tomorrow."

"Yes, please," she whispers, and then she runs her tongue across my bottom lip. "I want to feel you inside me, Rhett."

Then that's what you're going to get.

After pulling her panties all the way off, I lift her into my arms. She wraps her legs around my waist, moaning when my dick slides against her clit.

"You're so wet, sweetheart. Is all of that for me?"

"Yes," she says with a breathy exhale. She grinds against me, shuddering, and I squeeze her ass with my hands.

I walk toward her closed door, pressing her against it. Then I hold her with one hand, reaching between us and flicking her clit with my other.

"Fuck," she whispers. When I press small, gentle circles to it, her back arches. "Oh my god, Rhett."

Her reaction sends a burst of pride through me. I've never wanted to hear a woman say my name this much in my entire life. "Are you ready for me?" My words come out low in her ear. I suck the soft skin of her neck into mouth.

"Yes. Yes, I'm ready. Please."

When I finally sink into her, it's with a low groan. *Fuck,* she feels good. Why didn't I do this earlier this weekend?

Because you weren't ready yet.

She grips my arms, slowly rolling her hips to adjust. I slide in further, and she clenches around me.

"Am I hurting you?"

She shakes her head. "Just give me a second."

I nod, capturing her lips in a kiss. It deepens, and I work her clit gently while she moans my name into my mouth. She slips down another inch or two, taking all of me in, and she breaks our kiss with a gasp.

"I need you," she whispers, looking at me with such trust it makes my heart skip a beat. "Don't hold back, Rhett. Please. I never want to forget what you feel like."

Fuck me.

I pull out of her, leaving in just the tip, before slamming back inside her. She cries out, and for a moment I think I've gone too hard. But then she smiles.

"More."

So I give it to her. Her eyes roll into the back of her head, and it only makes me plow her into the door harder.

"Oh god—Rhett, I—I can't last—oh *fuck.*" She buries her face into my shoulder and screams.

I keep up my pace, drawing out her orgasm as I feel mine approaching. I didn't want it to end this quickly, but she's just too fucking perfect.

She's not going anywhere. You can savor it next time.

Wren moans as I bottom out inside of her over and over again. And as I get closer and closer, the tension building, her lips find mine in a passionate kiss.

"Fuck," I hiss out, slamming into her one more time before I finish. It's explosive, and addictive, and I don't think I'll ever get enough.

When I stop, Wren goes limp in my arms and rests her head on my shoulder. "Rhett," she whispers into my neck, panting. "That was—that was *so good.*"

I kiss her as a wave of exhaustion crashes over me. *Shit.* How did I get so tired so quickly? I still have to drive back home.

"I have to pee," Wren says.

I pull out of her, setting her down gently. As she disappears into the bathroom, I pull my clothes back on and collapse onto the bed.

My heartbeat is finally slowing, and I can't keep my eyes open.

The last thought I have is the realization that I must finally be crashing for the first time since Tuesday.

CHAPTER FIFTEEN

Wren

I frown at the snow falling outside. It's coming down hard and fast—enough that the thought of Rhett driving in it makes my stomach turn with unease. Sure, I may be more anxious than the average person, but this is *bad*.

"Hey, it's snowing pretty hard outside, I think—"

When I step into my bedroom, I find Rhett passed out on top of all my blankets. "You awake?" I whisper.

He doesn't stir.

My heart warms as I watch him breathing softly. He looks so peaceful, like everything that's weighing him down has finally disappeared.

I grab a spare blanket from the living room and drape it over him. Then I head back out of the room, grabbing my phone from the kitchen counter and calling Oliver.

"Hey, princess. Is everything okay?" I can hear him trying to hide the worry in his voice, but he's doing a poor job at it.

"We're fine," I say softly. "But, um, Rhett fell asleep."

"Oh, thank god," Oliver says. "He's not taking up your whole bed, is he? He has a bad habit of doing that."

I giggle. "No, he's not. But good to know."

"Sleep well, Wren." Oliver pauses as I hear Elliot say something I can't quite make out. "Ell says to call us if you need anything."

"I will, promise. Goodnight."

I leave the hall light on, as I always do, and then I crawl into bed. I keep my arm from underneath the covers, wrapping it around Rhett. His warmth seeps into my body, and I smile.

A chance.

That's what we all agreed to. A cautious start at adding me into their relationship. The thought of getting even more attached to them scares me, but it also causes butterflies to take off in my stomach.

Because what if it all works out? Elliot, Oliver, and Rhett all care for me so much. Hell, that's even the reason Elliot was willing to let me go, even though it hurt.

So I drift off to sleep with a light heart and a smile on my lips. Because even though I'm afraid to get hurt again, I know—I *know*—that these men will do everything possible to keep me.

And I'll do the same for them.

The story continues in Perfect Convergence.

Deleted Scene

If you want to read one of the deleted scenes from Blissful Masquerade, go to subscribepage.io/bm-bonus and sign up to my email list.

Author's Note

Thanks so much for reading Blissful Masquerade! Wren's story with these lovely men popped into my head in January 2022, and I had a blast writing it. Their story continues in Perfect Convergence, the second out of six books in the Ruthless Desires Series.

I've been writing since I was a teenager. Creating different story-worlds and characters was my absolute favorite pastime (okay, okay, coping mechanism). I've always loved romance, especially dark romance with a little suspense sprinkled in, so it's no surprise that it's what I ended up writing.

If you'd like to stay up to date with my latest writings and adventures, you can check out my website elirafirethorn.com or follow me on Instagram, Pinterest, and TikTok @elirafirethorn.

Also By Elira Firethorn

Dark Luxuries Trilogy

Deepest Obsession

Twisted Redemption

Darkest Retribution

Dark Luxuries Epilogue

Ruthless Desires Series

Blissful Masquerade

Perfect Convergence

Undying Resilience

Wretched Corruption

Standalones

Moonflower

Printed in Great Britain
by Amazon

34780453R00088